IN GHOSTLY COMPANY

IN GHOSTLY
COMPANY

Amyas Northcote

with an Introduction by
David Stuart Davies

WORDSWORTH EDITIONS

I

Readers interested in other titles from
Wordsworth Editions are invited to visit our
website at www.wordsworth-editions.com

For our latest list and a full mail-order service contact
Bibliophile Books, Unit 5 Datapoint,
South Crescent, London E16 4TL
Tel: +44 020 74 74 24 74
Fax: +44 020 74 74 85 89
orders@bibliophilebooks.com
www.bibliophilebooks.com

This edition published 2010 by
Wordsworth Editions Limited
8B East Street, Ware,
Hertfordshire SG12 9HJ

ISBN 978 1 84022 643 0

Typeset in Great Britain by Roperford Editorial
Printed by Clays Ltd, St Ives plc

CONTENTS

INTRODUCTION

The writing of ghost stories has attracted more talented amateurs than any other form of literature. By the term 'amateur', I mean those individuals whose main occupation in life is not writing, but those who take up their pen or sit at their typewriters in their idle hours between the demands of their normal profession. The list of candidates in the ghost story genre includes M. R. James, Sir Andrew Caldecott and A. C. and R. H. Benson. Another name to add to the list, one which is forgotten today by all but the most knowledgeable aficionado of supernatural fiction, is Amyas Northcote.

Northcote remains a shadowy figure, and not a great deal is known about him or what prompted him to create this delicious collection of ghost stories. He was born on 25 October 1864 into a privileged background. He was the seventh child of a successful politician, Sir Stafford Northcote who was lord of the manor at Pynes, situated a few miles from Exeter. During his childhood years, all the great Tory politicians, including Disraeli, Lord Salisbury and Randolph Churchill, were guests at the house. Sir Stafford was a great devotee of the theatre and literature. He had an especial fascination for ghost stories and the tales of the Arabian Nights and needed little encouragement to spin yarns of magic, wizardry and the fantastic to his children. No doubt this influenced the young Amyas Northcote in his reading tastes and sowed seeds of inspiration which were not to flower until many years later.

Amyas attended Eton and was there at the same time as that doyen of ghost story writers M. R. James. It is not known if the two young men knew each other at this time, but the ancient and academic atmosphere that they breathed in together finds its way into both of their writings. Amyas followed the typical route from Eton to one of the Oxbridge Universities: Oxford in his case. In his story 'Mr Mortimer's Diary' Northcote makes the following observation which could easily apply to himself.

> Mr Roger Mortimer was a gentleman born of well-to-do parents . . .
> and was educated according to the usual practice of well-to-do folk;
> Eton and Oxford claimed him . . .

Shortly after his father died in 1887, Amyas emigrated to America where he set up in business in Chicago and, in 1890, married Helen Mary Dudley, from Kentucky.

During this period he developed his talent for writing. These were journalistic pieces full of political comment and wry observations rather than fiction, but they revealed that he had the ability to present his ideas and opinions in a cool and deceptively unemotional fashion, which later became a stylistic feature of his ghost stories. His time in America was a happy one and he held great affection for the country and its people. In one of his newspaper articles he affirmed:

> The United States is my abiding place; my warmest friends are
> Americans . . . No foreigner who has not himself experienced it can
> be made to understand the kindness and hospitality with which
> Americans of all classes treat the stranger within their gates.

Northcote returned to England at the turn of the century, owning properties in London and the Chilterns. Little is known about his activities at this time except that he took on the role of Justice of the Peace in Buckinghamshire. Then, it would seem, out of the blue he brought out a collection of ghost stories in 1921. *In Ghostly Company* was published by John Lane, Bodley Head in November that year, just in time for Christmas, the season when it seems ghost stories come into their own.

The book received mixed reviews. The *Times Literary Supplement* referred to the author's 'unemotional style' but added 'in several of the stories, there is a subtle didactic touch which is not overdone.'

Indeed, the key words here are 'subtle' and 'unemotional'. If the reader is in search of stomach-churning, heart-stopping violent horror, he will not find it in the stories of Amyas Northcote. His style is most akin to that of M. R. James in the sense that it is measured and insidiously suggestive, producing unnerving chills rather than shocks and gasps. After reading Northcote's tales one is unsettled and disturbed. This is partly due to the fact that the hauntings or strange occurrences in his stories take place in natural or mundane surroundings – surroundings which would be familiar to most readers but ones never before thought of as unusual or threatening.

Consider for example the story 'In the Woods', which takes the form of a dream-like anecdote. It has no resolution and like many of Northcote's stories no explanation either. He does not follow the path of many ghost story writers by explaining why or how the haunting has taken place. To do that, he seems to suggest, removes much of the mystery and the fear. The real point of fear is that there is no rational explanation.

In essence, there is no plot to 'In the Woods'. The central character, a girl whose name we are never told, communes with nature and at first finds peace and tranquillity. 'The woods enthralled her' is a phrase used several times in the text and subtly the meaning of the word 'enthralled' changes from the implication of enchantment to enslavement. Northcote delicately and yet tangibly transforms this pastoral idyll into something dark and sinister. The woods become a character, and a threatening one at that: 'The firs stood dark and motionless, with a faint aspect of menace in their clustering ranks . . . '

Nature is a living thing with hidden undercurrents of danger.

Sadly *In Ghostly Company* proved to be Amyas Northcote's only collection of ghost stories – his only published volume of any kind in fact. It has been suggested that it was his family name and his connections that persuaded the original publisher to accept the book. Certainly a slim volume of ghost stories by an unknown author was not going to make them a huge profit, but we shall never know the truth regarding this theory.

Amyas Northcote died very suddenly just eighteen months after the collection was published and no further stories were found amongst his papers. It is perhaps because of this brief flare on the literary scene, this limited contribution to the genre, that the book as a whole was neglected for so long. The publishers, not able to build up a readership for the author because of his untimely death, paid little attention to the volume and never republished. It was only because certain stories, 'Brickett Bottom' in particular, found their way into various anthologies, that Northcote's name was remembered at all.

'Brickett Bottom' was championed by the great supernatural scholar Montague Summers who featured it in his classic *The Supernatural Omnibus* in 1931. It is typical of Northcote's approach to the ghost story. It features, as several of his other tales do, a disappearance. It is a simple tale set in the seemingly harmless lush English countryside but before the reader is fully aware of it, the author has begun to build the tension and suspense. One of the major commentators on the British ghost story, Jack Adrian, thought that 'Brickett Bottom' ' . . . is far, far better than simply a good tale well told . . . it plumbs the most profound depths of horror and despair'. Adrian maintains that 'there are a good many giants of the genre from that golden late-Victorian, Edwardian and Georgian period, who never wrote anything half as excellent.'

Another story that features a disappearance is 'The Picture'. This tale is particularly Jamesian in style with all its historical detail and takes Northcote away from his typical *mis en scène* of the English countryside to Hungary. Here we are given a wicked Count and an old castle as elements in this tale of cruel love.

Like 'Brickett Bottom', another tale favoured by admirers of Northcote's work, appearing in several anthologies over the years, is 'The Late Mrs Fowkes'. This story is perhaps the least typical of Northcote's output as it is concerned with witchcraft. It features a ceremony of Devil-worship very reminiscent of a scene in Dennis Wheatley's classic *The Devil Rides Out* which was first published in 1934. It is not beyond the bounds of possibility, maybe probability, that Wheatley, who was an aficionado of supernatural fiction, was familiar with this story and, shall we say, influenced by it and the Devil-worshipping scene in particular.

Northcote had the ability to take a moment, an incident, and invest it with a strangeness that at once seems inevitable and yet suddenly surprisingly frightening in its potential. For example 'The Downs' presents what appears to be a most mundane scenario: a man walks over the Downs as darkness falls to return to his lodgings. There is a long and seemingly inconsequential preamble before the narrator actually sets off on his journey, which lulls us into thinking that this is a very tame story. However, there are clues dropped casually into the text to alert the reader to the unpleasantness to come, like the observation that, 'I was perfectly confident in my ability to find my way back over the Downs to Branksome at night as the path was very familiar to us, and I expected to be aided by the light of the moon which would rise about ten o'clock.' This innocent, naïve belief is juxtaposed shortly afterwards by confession that, 'Up to this night, I had never in the least suspected that I was possessed of any special psychic intelligence.' These two statements inform the astute and imaginative reader that we are about to witness some very strange occurrences. Without preparing us for precisely what the narrator will encounter on his late-night journey, Northcote has clearly implied that something disturbing *will* happen. As it does. Out of a simple situation comes mystery and frightening consequences.

Northcote applies a similar approach in 'The Steps' which begins with the assertion that, 'The following story purports to be the actual experience of one of our leading medical men.' So much is packed into that statement: the word 'purports' suggests that that there are elements of this tale which we may have difficulty believing; the word 'actual' increases that sense that what we are about to read will be difficult to believe; but then he adds that the person at the centre of the story 'is a leading medical man', a character with a respectable practical scientific background who is most unlikely to have an impressionable imagination. Northcote strengthens the idea that what he is telling us is really the truth by presenting the incidents as creepy rather than sensational so that we can hear and believe in those haunted footsteps.

In some stories, such as 'Mr Mortimer's Diary' and 'Mr Kershaw and Mr Wilcox' – both, incidentally involving a feud between two men, one of whom believes he has been wronged – Northcote plays with the reader, presenting events that could simply be the result of a disturbed mind. It is possible that it is the power of guilt and the force of imagination that causes the strange outcome rather than a supernatural experience.

Northcote's technique of relaxing the reader early in the story before reaching the nerve-tingling moments, as mentioned in the comments referring to 'The Downs', is carried out in many of the stories using different methods. However, none is more cunning than his ploy in 'The Young Lady in Black'. In this tale, the author states at the outset that while it is not 'a tale of horror and woe, like the typical ghost story, still it is interesting as opening up for consideration the question of whether, after the death of a body, the spirit is able to carry on and bring to a more or less satisfactory conclusion some task commenced in the flesh.' The prose may be cool and unemotional but nevertheless it acts as a hook to draw the reader in. The premise expressed in this apparently simple statement is in fact very frightening and tinged with horror.

The idea of the dead influencing the living is also found in 'The Late Earl of D.' in which Northcote takes the clever notion of the image of an evil deed surviving in an ethereal form long after its execution. The narrator sees a reflection in a darkened window which reveals a terrible truth.

So, in this fascinating volume we have a very varied confectionery of excellent ghost stories, which at first mislead with their 'unemotional style' but which eventually leave the reader with uneasy feelings and a surprising tingle of fear. This rare collection has long been out of print and is a very welcome addition to this series of all that is best and wonderful in the mystery and supernatural genre. Enjoy!

DAVID STUART DAVIES

IN GHOSTLY COMPANY

Brickett Bottom

The Reverend Arthur Maydew was the hard-working incumbent of a large parish in one of our manufacturing towns. He was also a student and a man of no strong physique, so that when an opportunity was presented to him to take an annual holiday by exchanging parsonages with an elderly clergyman, Mr Roberts, the puarson of the Parish of Overbury, and an acquaintance of his own, he was glad to avail himself of it.

Overbury is a small and very remote village in one of our most lovely and rural counties, and Mr Roberts had long held the living of it.

Without further delay we can transport Mr Maydew and his family, which consisted only of two daughters, to their temporary home. The two young ladies, Alice and Maggie, the heroines of this narrative, were at that time aged twenty-six and twenty-four years respectively. Both of them were attractive girls, fond of such society as they could find in their own parish and, the former especially, always pleased to extend the circle of their acquaintance. Although the elder in years, Alice in many ways yielded place to her sister, who was the more energetic and practical and upon whose shoulders the bulk of the family cares and responsibilities rested. Alice was inclined to be absent-minded and emotional and to devote more of her thoughts and time to speculations of an abstract nature than her sister.

Both of the girls, however, rejoiced at the prospect of a period of quiet and rest in a pleasant country neighbourhood, and both were gratified at knowing that their father would find in Mr Roberts's library much that would entertain his mind, and in Mr Roberts's garden an opportunity to indulge freely in his favourite game of croquet. They would have no doubt preferred some cheerful neighbours, but Mr Roberts was positive in his assurances that there was no one in the neighbourhood whose acquaintance would be of interest to them.

The first few weeks of their new life passed pleasantly for the Maydew family. Mr Maydew quickly gained renewed vigour in his quiet and congenial surroundings, and in the delightful air, while his daughters spent much of their time in long walks about the country and in exploring its beauties.

One evening late in August the two girls were returning from a long walk along one of their favourite paths, which led along the side of the Downs. On their right, as they walked, the ground fell away sharply to a narrow glen, named Brickett Bottom, about three-quarters of a mile in length, along the bottom of which ran a little-used country road leading to a farm, known as Blaise's Farm, and then onward and upward to lose itself as a sheep track on the higher Downs. On their side of the slope some scattered trees and bushes grew, but beyond the lane and running up over the farther slope of the glen was a thick wood, which extended away to Carew Court, the seat of a neighbouring magnate, Lord Carew. On their left the open Down rose above them and beyond its crest lay Overbury.

The girls were walking hastily, as they were later than they had intended to be and were anxious to reach home. At a certain point at which they had now arrived the path forked, the right hand branch leading down into Brickett Bottom and the left hand turning up over the Down to Overbury.

Just as they were about to turn into the left hand path Alice suddenly stopped and pointing downwards exclaimed: 'How very curious, Maggie! Look, there is a house down there in the Bottom, which we have, or at least I have, never noticed before, often as we have walked up the Bottom.'

Maggie followed with her eyes her sister's pointing finger. 'I don't see any house,' she said.

'Why, Maggie,' said her sister, 'can't you see it! A quaint-looking, old-fashioned red brick house, there just where the road bends to the right. It seems to be standing in a nice, well-kept garden too.'

Maggie looked again, but the light was beginning to fade in the glen and she was short-sighted to boot.

'I certainly don't see anything,' she said. 'but then I am so blind and the light is getting bad; yes, perhaps I do see a house,' she added, straining her eyes.

'Well, it is there,' replied her sister, 'and tomorrow we will come and explore it.'

Maggie agreed readily enough, and the sisters went home, still speculating on how they had happened not to notice the house before and resolving firmly on an expedition thither the next day. However, the expedition did not come off as planned, for that evening Maggie slipped on the stairs and fell, spraining her ankle in such a fashion as to preclude walking for some time.

Notwithstanding the accident to her sister, Alice remained possessed by the idea of making further investigations into the house she had looked down upon from the hill the evening before; and the next day, having seen Maggie carefully settled for the afternoon, she started off for Brickett Bottom. She returned in triumph and much intrigued over her discoveries, which she eagerly narrated to her sister.

Yes. There was a nice, old-fashioned red brick house, not very large and set in a charming, old-world garden in the Bottom. It stood on a tongue of land jutting out from the woods, just at the point where the lane, after a fairly straight course from its junction with the main road half a mile away, turned sharply to the right in the direction of Blaise's Farm. More than that, Alice had seen the people of the house, whom she described as an old gentleman and a lady, presumably his wife. She had not clearly made out the gentleman, who was sitting in the porch, but the old lady, who had been in the garden busy with her flowers, had looked up and smiled pleasantly at her as she passed. She was sure, she said, that they were nice people and that it would be pleasant to make their acquaintance.

Maggie was not quite satisfied with Alice's story. She was of a more prudent and retiring nature than her sister; she had an uneasy feeling that, if the old couple had been desirable or attractive neighbours, Mr Roberts would have mentioned them, and knowing Alice's nature she said what she could to discourage her vague idea of endeavouring to make acquaintance with the owners of the red brick house.

On the following morning, when Alice came to her sister's room to enquire how she did, Maggie noticed that she looked pale and rather absent-minded, and, after a few commonplace remarks had passed, she asked: 'What is the matter, Alice? You don't look yourself this morning.'

Her sister gave a slightly embarrassed laugh. 'Oh, I am all right,' she replied, 'only I did not sleep very well. I kept on dreaming about the house. It was such an odd dream too; the house seemed to be home, and yet to be different.'

'What, that house in Brickett Bottom?' said Maggie. 'Why, what is the matter with you, you seem to be quite crazy about the place?'

'Well, it is curious, isn't it, Maggie, that we should have only just discovered it, and that it looks to be lived in by nice people? I wish we could get to know them.'

Maggie did not care to resume the argument of the night before and the subject dropped, nor did Alice again refer to the house or its inhabitants for some little time. In fact, for some days the weather was wet and Alice was forced to abandon her walks, but when the weather once more became fine she resumed them, and Maggie suspected that Brickett Bottom formed one of her sister's favourite expeditions. Maggie became anxious over her sister, who seemed to grow daily more absent-minded and silent, but she refused to be drawn into any confidential talk, and Maggie was nonplussed.

One day, however, Alice returned from her afternoon walk in an unusually excited state of mind, of which Maggie sought an explanation. It came with a rush. Alice said that, that afternoon, as she approached the house in Brickett Bottom, the old lady, who as usual was busy in her garden, had walked down to the gate as she passed and had wished her good day.

Alice had replied and, pausing, a short conversation had followed. Alice could not remember the exact tenor of it, but, after she had paid a compliment to the old lady's flowers, the latter had rather diffidently asked her to enter the garden for a closer view. Alice had hesitated, and the old lady had said 'Don't be afraid of me, my dear, I like to see young ladies about me and my husband finds their society quite necessary to him.' After a pause she went on: 'Of course nobody has told you about us. My husband is Colonel Paxton, late of the Indian Army, and we have been here for many, many years. It's rather lonely, for so few people ever see us. Do come in and meet the Colonel.'

'I hope you didn't go in,' said Maggie rather sharply.

'Why not?' replied Alice.

'Well, I don't like Mrs Paxton asking you in that way,' answered Maggie.

'I don't see what harm there was in the invitation,' said Alice. 'I didn't go in because it was getting late and I was anxious to get home; but – '

'But what?' asked Maggie.

Alice shrugged her shoulders. 'Well,' she said, 'I have accepted Mrs Paxton's invitation to pay her a little visit tomorrow.' And she gazed defiantly at Maggie.

Maggie became distinctly uneasy on hearing of this resolution. She did not like the idea of her impulsive sister visiting people on such slight acquaintance, especially as they had never heard them mentioned before. She endeavoured by all means, short of appealing to Mr Maydew, to dissuade her sister from going, at any rate until there had been time to make some enquiries as to the Paxtons. Alice, however, was obdurate.

What harm could happen to her? she asked. Mrs Paxton was a charming old lady. She was going early in the afternoon for a short visit. She would be back for tea and croquet with her father and, anyway, now that Maggie was laid up, long solitary walks were unendurable and she was not going to let slip the chance of following up what promised to be a pleasant acquaintance.

Maggie could do nothing more. Her ankle was better and she was able to get down to the garden and sit in a long chair near her father, but walking was still quite out of the question, and it was with some misgivings that on the following day she watched Alice depart gaily for her visit, promising to be back by half-past four at the very latest.

The afternoon passed quietly till nearly five, when Mr Maydew, looking up from his book, noticed Maggie's uneasy expression and asked: 'Where is Alice?'

'Out for a walk,' replied Maggie; and then after a short pause she went on: 'And she has also gone to pay a call on some neighbours whom she has recently discovered.'

'Neighbours,' ejaculated Mr Maydew, 'what neighbours? Mr Roberts never spoke of any neighbours to me.'

'Well, I don't know much about them,' answered Maggie. 'Only Alice and I were out walking the day of my accident and saw – or at least she saw, for I am so blind I could not quite make it out – a house in Brickett Bottom. The next day she went to look at it closer, and yesterday she told me that she had made the acquaintance of the people living in it. She says that they are a retired Indian officer and his wife, a Colonel and Mrs Paxton, and Alice describes Mrs Paxton as a charming old lady, who pressed her to come and see them. So she has gone this afternoon, but she promised me she would be back long before this.'

Mr Maydew was silent for a moment and then said: 'I am not well pleased about this. Alice should not be so impulsive and scrape acquaintance with absolutely unknown people. Had there been nice neighbours in Brickett Bottom, I am certain Mr Roberts would have told us.'

The conversation dropped; but both father and daughter were disturbed and uneasy and, tea having been finished and the clock striking half-past five, Mr Maydew asked Maggie: 'When did you say Alice would be back?'

'Before half-past four at the latest, father.'

'Well, what can she be doing? What can have delayed her? You say you did not see the house,' he went on.

'No,' said Maggie, 'I cannot say I did. It was getting dark and you know how short-sighted I am.'

'But surely you must have seen it at some other time,' said her father.

'That is the strangest part of the whole affair,' answered Maggie. 'We have often walked up the Bottom, but I never noticed the house, nor had Alice till that evening. I wonder,' she went on after a short pause, 'if it would not be well to ask Smith to harness the pony and drive over to bring her back. I am not happy about her – I am afraid –'

'Afraid of what?' said her father in the irritated voice of a man who is growing frightened. 'What can have gone wrong in this quiet place? Still, I'll send Smith over for her.'

So saying he rose from his chair and sought out Smith, the rather dull-witted gardener-groom attached to Mr Roberts's service.

'Smith,' he said,' I want you to harness the pony at once and go over to Colonel Paxton's in Brickett Bottom and bring Miss Maydew home.'

The man stared at him. 'Go where, sir?' he said.

Mr Maydew repeated the order and the man, still staring stupidly, answered: 'I never heard of Colonel Paxton, sir. I don't know what house you mean.'

Mr Maydew was now growing really anxious. 'Well, harness the pony at once,' he said; and going back to Maggie he told her of what he called Smith's stupidity, and asked her if she felt that her ankle would be strong enough to permit her to go with him and Smith to the Bottom to point out the house.

Maggie agreed readily and in a few minutes the party started off. Brickett Bottom, although not more than three-quarters of a mile away over the Downs, was at least three miles by road; and as it was nearly six o'clock before Mr Maydew left the Vicarage, and the pony was old and slow, it was getting late before the entrance to Brickett Bottom was reached. Turning into the lane the cart proceeded slowly up the Bottom, Mr Maydew and Maggie looking anxiously from side to side, whilst Smith drove stolidly on looking neither to time right nor left.

'Where is the house?' said Mr Maydew presently.

'At the bend of the road,' answered Maggie, her heart sickening as she looked out through the failing light to see the trees stretching their ranks in unbroken formation along it. The cart reached the bend. 'It should be here,' whispered Maggie.

They pulled up. Just in front of them the road bent to the right round a tongue of land, which, unlike the rest of the right hand side of the road, was free from trees and was covered only by rough grass and stray bushes. A closer inspection disclosed evident signs of terraces having once been formed on it, but of a house there was no trace.

'Is this the place?' said Mr Maydew in a low voice.

Maggie nodded.

'But there is no house here,' said her father. 'What does it all mean? Are you sure of yourself, Maggie? Where is Alice?'

Before Maggie could answer a voice was heard calling 'Father! Maggie!' The sound of the voice was thin and high and, paradoxically, it sounded both very near and yet as if it came from some infinite distance. The cry was thrice repeated and then silence fell. Mr Maydew and Maggie stared at each other.

'That was Alice's voice,' said Mr Maydew huskily, 'she is near and in trouble, and is calling us. Which way did you think it came from, Smith?' he added, turning to the gardener.

'I didn't hear anybody calling,' said the man.

'Nonsense!' answered Mr Maydew.

And then he and Maggie both began to call 'Alice. Alice. Where are you?'

There was no reply and Mr Maydew sprang from the cart, at the same time bidding Smith to hand the reins to Maggie and come and search for the missing girl. Smith obeyed him and both men, scrambling up the turfy bit of ground, began to search and call through the neighbouring wood. They heard and saw nothing, however, and after an agonised search Mr Maydew ran down to the cart and begged Maggie to drive on to Blaise's Farm for help leaving himself and Smith to continue the search.

Maggie followed her father's instructions and was fortunate enough to find Mr Rumbold, the farmer, his two sons and a couple of labourers just returning from the harvest field. She explained what had happened, and the farmer and his men promptly volunteered to form a search party, though Maggie, in spite of her anxiety, noticed a queer expression on Mr Rumbold's face as she told him her tale.

The party, provided with lanterns, now went down the Bottom, joined Mr Maydew and Smith and made an exhaustive but absolutely fruitless search of the woods near the bend of the road. No trace of the missing girl was to be found, and after a long and anxious time the search was abandoned, one of the young Rumbolds volunteering to ride into the nearest town and notify the police.

Maggie, though with little hope in her own heart, endeavoured to cheer her father on their homeward way with the idea that Alice might have returned to Overbury over the Downs whilst they were going by road to the Bottom, and that she had seen them and called to them in jest when they were opposite the tongue of land.

However, when they reached home there was no Alice and, though the next day the search was resumed and full inquiries were instituted by the police, all was to no purpose. No trace of Alice was ever found, the last human being that saw her having been an old woman, who had met her going down the path into the Bottom on the afternoon of her disappearance, and who described her as smiling but looking 'queerlike'.

This is the end of the story, but the following may throw some light upon it.

The history of Alice's mysterious disappearance became widely known through the medium of the Press and Mr Roberts, distressed beyond measure at what had taken place, returned in all haste to Overbury to offer what comfort and help he could give to his afflicted friend and tenant. He called upon the Maydews and, having heard their tale, sat for a short time in silence. Then he said: 'Have you ever heard any local gossip concerning this Colonel and Mrs Paxton?'

'No,' replied Mr Maydew, 'I never heard their names until the day of my poor daughter's fatal visit.'

'Well,' said Mr Roberts, 'I will tell you all I can about them, which is not very much, I fear.' He paused and then went on: 'I am now nearly seventy-five years old, and for nearly seventy years no house has stood in Brickett Bottom. But when I was a child of about five there was an old-fashioned, red brick house standing in a garden at the bend of the road, such as you have described. It was owned and lived in by a retired Indian soldier and his wife, a Colonel and Mrs Paxton. At the time I speak of, certain events having taken place at the house and the old couple having died, it was sold by their heirs to Lord Carew, who shortly after pulled it down on the ground that it interfered with his shooting. Colonel and Mrs Paxton were well known to my father, who was the clergyman here before me, and to the neighbourhood in general. They lived quietly and were not unpopular, but the Colonel was supposed to possess a violent and vindictive temper. Their family consisted only of themselves, their daughter and a couple of servants, the Colonel's old Army servant and his Eurasian wife. Well, I cannot tell you details of what happened, I was only a child; my father never liked gossip and in later years, when he talked to me on the subject, he always avoided any appearance of exaggeration or sensationalism. However, it is known that Miss Paxton fell in love with and became engaged to a young man to whom her parents took a strong dislike. They used every possible means to break off the match, and many rumours were set on foot as to their conduct – undue influence, even cruelty were charged against them. I do not know the truth, all I can say is that Miss Paxton died and a very bitter feeling against her parents sprang up. My father, however, continued to call, but was rarely admitted. In fact, he never saw Colonel Paxton after his daughter's death and only saw Mrs Paxton once or twice. He described her as an utterly broken woman, and was not surprised at her following her daughter to the grave in about three months' time. Colonel Paxton became, if possible, more of a recluse than ever after his wife's death and himself died not more than a month after her under circumstances which pointed to suicide. Again a crop of rumours sprang up, but there was no one in particular to take action, the doctor certified Death from Natural Causes, and Colonel Paxton, like his wife and daughter, was buried in this churchyard. The property passed to a distant relative, who came down to it for one night shortly afterwards; he never came again, having apparently conceived a violent dislike to the place, but arranged to pension off the servants and then sold the house to Lord Carew, who was glad to purchase this little island in the middle of his property. He pulled it down soon after he had bought it, and the garden was left to relapse into a wilderness.'

Mr Roberts paused. 'Those are all the facts,' he added.

'But there is something more,' said Maggie.

Mr Roberts hesitated for a while. 'You have a right to know all,' he said almost to himself; then louder he continued: 'What I am now going to tell you is really rumour, vague and uncertain; I cannot fathom its truth or its meaning. About five years after the house had been pulled down a young maidservant at Carew Court was out walking one afternoon. She was a stranger to the village and a newcomer to the Court. On returning home to tea she told her fellow-servants that as she walked down Brickett Bottom, which place she described clearly, she passed a red brick house at the bend of the road and that a kind-faced old lady had asked her to step in for a while. She did not go in, not because she had any suspicions of there being anything uncanny, but simply because she feared to be late for tea.

'I do not think she ever visited the Bottom again and she had no other similar experience, so far as I am aware.

'Two or three years later, shortly after my father's death, a travelling tinker with his wife and daughter camped for the night at the foot of the Bottom. The girl strolled away up the glen to gather blackberries and was never seen or heard of again. She was searched for in vain – of course, one does not know the truth – and she may have run away voluntarily from her parents, although there was no known cause for her doing so.

'That,' concluded Mr Roberts, 'is all I can tell you of either facts or rumours; all that I can now do is to pray for you and for her.'

Mr Kershaw and Mr Wilcox

The relations between Mr Kershaw and Mr Wilcox were somewhat closer than merely those of business connections and yet were not sufficiently close to be dignified by the name of friendship. The two men were neighbours, living in similar houses, each standing apart in its own garden, in one of our more exclusive London suburbs and were acquaintances of many years standing. They were both men of middle age. Mr Kershaw was a married man with three children; Mr Wilcox was a bachelor.

In appearance and in character the two men were widely dissimilar. Mr Kershaw was a powerfully built, well-preserved man, warm-hearted, cheerful and sanguine in temperament. He possessed considerable ability and his active mind teemed with schemes and ideas, some of which held good promise of success, if carefully worked out, though many were hopelessly impracticable. In support of his various business ventures and projects he had adventured more than the somewhat slender fortune to which he had fallen heir justified, and he was continually seeking means whereby he could raise further capital to promote the success of his beloved projects. In fact he was a type of what may be called the mortgagor mind, the mind that can foresee no obstacles as insuperable and that, venturing too much, frequently loses all.

Mr Wilcox was of a very different temperament and may be fairly set down as of the mortgagee type. He was a cautious, shrewd and able lender, ready to promote the success of an enterprise, provided always that he ran no risk thereby, and equally ready to wreck either the business or its promoters' fortunes did he see any sure and substantial gain for himself in the process. Left by his parents the heir to a moderate fortune, by strict attention to business methods as outlined above, he had succeeded in turning himself into a wealthy man. Withal he was outwardly of a jovial turn, a good storyteller and a hearty fellow, fond of good food and the luxuries of life and possessed of a large acquaintance among his neighbours, with whom, as a rule, he did not engage in business affairs and who knew him chiefly as a pleasant companion. In person he was of middle height, bald and extremely fat, in fact, the very antithesis of Mr Kershaw's athletic and well-conserved frame. The date of this story is about ten years ago and the time late summer, when most of the business world is seeking relaxation far from town. Neither Mr Kershaw nor Mr Wilcox, for reasons which will soon become apparent, was taking such repose from toil, but Mr Kershaw had sent his wife and family to the seaside and was, therefore, a bachelor in his own house, cared for by a reduced number of servants.

With this preface the heart of the story may now be approached. For some time past the affairs of Mr Kershaw had not been going well. One after another, schemes on which he had counted as money makers had failed and been abandoned; until now, of all his various enterprises, only one was left. But on the success of this one he confidently relied, and the remainder of his whole future was bound up in it. Successful, it would bring him honour and wealth; its non-success would involve him in hopeless bankruptcy. There was no reason, however, to dread failure. Experts who had investigated the invention had pronounced unanimously in its favour. The demand for the appliance would be great, it would satisfy a popular need. There was only one difficulty to be overcome, and that was the provision of certain further capital to place the business upon an absolutely sound footing. This difficulty, however, did not seriously trouble Mr Kershaw, because, was he not dealing with his friend, Mr Wilcox?

Some time before he had, in his usual expansive fashion, discussed his incipient invention with that gentleman, and Mr Wilcox, quick to recognise any opportunity for adding to his fortune, had entered into an agreement with him, whereby Mr Wilcox agreed to lend upon security – which security included the patents and models of the new invention – up to a certain amount in cash for the development of the idea, taking one half of the prospective profits, Mr Kershaw retaining the other half for himself.

Well, Wilcox had carried out his side of the bargain, the money had all been spent, and now a little more was required of course Wilcox would be reasonable and see to that. 'Good fellow, Wilcox,' thought Mr Kershaw, as he went over to his neighbour's house one afternoon to discuss the position. Alas, Mr Kershaw did not know, as he had thought he did, his Wilcox, even after years of acquaintance.

He laid the whole position clearly and candidly before Mr Wilcox and wound up by explaining the necessity for some further cash advances, advances which, as he truly said, were certain to be repaid and which were necessary to protect the whole of the work arid money that had already been expended.

Mr Wilcox listened in absolute and ominous silence. At last Mr Kershaw had done and awaited his reply. It came – and was brief and to the point. Mr Wilcox would not put up another penny: he was very sorry, but he was very firm. More than that he plainly told Mr Kershaw that he meant to insist on his rights. Mr Kershaw had had his money on loan, he had paid no interest thereon, matters at the works were in a mess, he was going to foreclose on the lien he had taken over factory, invention, everything. Perhaps the invention was a good one, that remained to be seen, but the first thing he meant to do was to take entire possession of it.

Mr Kershaw was dumbfounded. 'But what about me?' he asked. 'Do you know that all I have is staked on this business? If I lose that, I lose everything.'

'I am sorry, Kershaw,' said the other. 'But business is business, and I must protect myself.'

'Give me time at least,' cried the unhappy Mr Kershaw. 'Give me a chance to raise the money I owe you elsewhere, and pay you off.'

'I cannot agree to that,' replied Mr Wilcox. 'That was not the bargain between us. Remember, our agreement provided for my retaining my half interest.'

Mr Kershaw began to lose control of himself. 'You dog,' he cried, 'you know there is a fortune in it and you want to take advantage of me and get it all.'

Mr Wilcox smiled. 'You can form what opinion you like of me,' he said, and then went on, 'You called me dog; call me top dog, that will be more correct.'

Mr Kershaw was beside himself. He argued, implored, threatened: Mr Wilcox remained cool and unmoved.

When, at last, exhausted, Mr Kershaw stopped, Mr Wilcox said: 'Have you quite finished? Good. Well, I may as well tell you that I wrote to my solicitors today instructing them to commence proceedings. I think we may as well close this interview now; your legal advisers will hear from my people shortly. Good afternoon.'

In a frenzy of rage and despair, Mr Kershaw left Mr Wilcox's house and sought his own. The blow had been so sudden, so utterly unexpected, that he was almost too stunned to think. He entered his own house and tried to collect himself, but his brain whirled.

Dinner was announced and mechanically he went to the dining-room; but he could not eat. Instead he drank heavily and, after going through the form of dining, stumbled into his study and sank into an easy chair.

What had happened to him? Gradually he began to collect his thoughts and the full horror of his position rushed over him. He was utterly and hopelessly ruined. He was in debt to his bankers, his very house was mortgaged up to the hilt. He had staked all, all on this one last enterprise. Success had been in his grasp and now all was gone, gone through his trust in Wilcox – Wilcox, who had just proved himself to be an unutterable scoundrel, and he cursed him long and bitterly. Wilcox had stolen his invention, Wilcox would make a fortune out of it, Wilcox would stand and jeer at him as he sank into the pit of failure and want. He and his family, his innocent family! His mind reeled at the thought of their distress and misery: to calm himself ho commenced to drink again. Still his mind worked fever-ishly. Was there nothing he could do, no one he could appeal to? He could think of nothing; the very fact of the holiday season being on rendered it even more hopeless. Everyone who might have helped him was away and there was no time to wait; that devil, Wilcox, had already begun proceedings. Well, Wilcox would burn in hell for this piece of work, even though he should profit by it on earth. But, all at once, a thought struck him: need Wilcox profit by it? Suppose God should kill him that very night and send his wicked soul shrieking to the Pit. Why not? That would be justice. But Justice needs an implement, why should he not kill Wilcox? Such a one was not fit to live. All the ranks of those whom Wilcox had oppressed would rise up and bless their deliverer. Heaven itself would approve his act! He thought again and again of what he might do: he seemed to see before him Mr Wilcox's puffy face, distorted in death, to feel Mr Wilcox's fat figure writhing in his grip. He rejoiced at the thought. Yes, he would kill Wilcox.

Almost before he knew it, he found himself standing on his own lawn. He glanced up at his own house; it was dark and silent, the whole suburb was silent, the night was silent. All was dark and silent; he crossed his lawn and bounded lightly over the fence dividing his own from Mr Wilcox's garden and looked up at Mr Wilcox's house. All there was dark and silent, save for a light in one window, the window which he knew to be that of Mr Wilcox's bedroom. So the dog was not yet asleep; did he know what was coming to him? Mr Kershaw stole towards the house. Without surprise he found the French window of the drawing-room open. God was helping him; He wished him to kill Wilcox. Softly he entered the room, softly he crossed it and glided up the stairs to the bedroom. His feet made no sound on the thick carpet. He reached the bedroom door, the handle turned easily in his grasp. He entered the room.

Mr Wilcox was not in bed. He was undressed and was seated in an armchair near the window, his pyjamas open at the neck on account of the heat. He looked up as the other entered.

'Kershaw,' he said in a low voice, 'what do you want?'

Mr Kershaw crossed the room quickly and stood over the other.

'I give you one more chance,' he said. 'Renew our old agreement, cancel your lawyer's letter, provide more money, or – '

He was going on when Mr Wilcox looking coolly at him broke in: 'Too late, my dear – '

Mr Kershaw did not wait for the end of the sentence. He sprang on Mr Wilcox, gripping his fat neck in his sinewy hands. The other struggled to rise, to repel his assailant, but he was as a child in Mr Kershaw's powerful grasp. Silently the struggle proceeded, but Mr Wilcox's movements grew fainter, his bulging eyes started from his head, his red face grew black, his limbs grew rigid and then relaxed. Still Mr Kershaw gripped his throat, and it was not till long after all motion had ceased that he finally relinquished his hold and let the poor body fall, a tumbled, broken heap, across the arm of the chair.

Then slowly he turned, went to the door, looked again at the motionless form, said 'Thank God,' and went out.

Mr Kershaw did not know how he got home, it seemed to him but a moment from the time he left Mr Wilcox's room to the time he found himself once more sitting in his own chair.

For a time he remained motionless and almost unconscious and then slowly the realisation of what he had done began to flow over him. He did not regret it: on the contrary he rejoiced, the world was rid of a scoundrel. Yes, he had killed Wilcox, he had gone to his house, he had given him a chance to repent. Wilcox had not taken it, so he had killed, had murdered – Stop, that was an ugly word, murder. Suddenly he visualised himself – he was a murderer, and the law, the law hanged murderers. He broke into a cold sweat of fear, every instant his own position became clearer. What had he done?

He had not benefited himself or his family, he still was deprived of his invention; ruin still stared him in the face and upon ruin he had piled disgrace, his wife would be the widow and his children the orphans of a murderer. Agony possessed his soul and he writhed in hopeless anguish. Gradually, however, he became calmer. He was a murderer, but why should murder out? If he could summon up courage and coolness enough to go on with his life undisturbed, why should he be found out? He must be cool and collected, he must act as he normally did.

He grew steadily calmer and laid out the line of his action. First he must go to bed and go noiselessly, so as not to let his household know he had been up so late. He slipped upstairs, undressed, lay down and waited for the day.

*   *   *

At the usual hour the maid knocked at his door. Mr Kershaw answered her as naturally as he could, and lay waiting to hear her say something of the dreadful tragedy next door. Surely by this time servants' gossip would have reached his house. But the girl said nothing and Mr Kershaw rose, bathed, dressed and went to his dining-room. Breakfast was ready; he could not eat, but he drank his coffee and waited for news.

None came, the household was undisturbed as ever. Mr Kershaw rose and peered out of the window at the Wilcox house. There was no sign of disturbance there either. What could have happened? At this moment his own door-bell rang. Mr Kershaw started violently. Was it the police already? He hurried into the front room and, looking out of the window, saw a man on his doorstep. The man had his back towards him, but Mr Kershaw saw at once he was a stranger and in ordinary civilian clothes.

A few moments later the maid announced: 'A gentleman to see you, sir.'

The man entered quietly behind her, and Mr Kershaw saw that his first judgment had been correct and that he was a stranger, although just for an instant his appearance recalled to him the look of his brother, to whom he had been passionately devoted, and who had died some ten years before.

The stranger bowed slightly, saying: 'Mr Kershaw, I believe?'

Mr Kershaw nodded, he was too agitated to speak. Who was this man and what did he want?

The other continued, disregarding the chair to which Mr Kershaw pointed: 'I have come at some inconvenience to myself on an errand to you, Mr Kershaw. I wish to tell you that you will find it greatly to your advantage to call without delay on Mr Wilcox.'

Mr Kershaw was stupefied with amazement. At last he managed to ejaculate: 'Call on Mr Wilcox!'

'Yes,' returned the stranger, 'and as soon as possible.'

'Who are you,' exclaimed Mr Kershaw, 'and why do you come with this message to me? I cannot call on Mr Wilcox. He is – ' he stopped himself in time. 'We have quarrelled,' he added lamely.

'My name is not important,' answered the other, 'but I come as a friend and I urge you to follow my advice; I know of your quarrel, but quarrels can be made up.'

Mr Kershaw's mind was labouring like a mill, but the idea suddenly flashed over him that this might be Wilcox's solicitor, who, ashamed of his client's action, was now seeking to repair the breach between him and himself.

'I can never make up with Mr Wilcox,' he said, 'it is too late.'

The stranger bowed. 'I have given my message,' he said. 'Think it over and act upon it.' Without another word he turned and left the room.

Almost as he closed the door the recollection of what he had said flashed across Mr Kershaw. 'It is too late'; he had given himself away, he was a lost man. He sprang from his chair and rushed into the hall. The stranger was not there.

'Mary,' he cried, 'has that gentleman gone?'

'Isn't he with you, sir?' said the maid. 'I didn't see him go out.'

Mr Kershaw hurried to the front door and went out into the road, at that hour nearly empty of traffic. He gazed up and down: the stranger was not to be seen. Crushed by the sense of his own folly and dumbfounded at the amazing message, Mr Kershaw returned to his study and endeavoured to think out his position.

Clearly the stranger knew something, but what and how much and why did he adopt this friendly attitude? Perhaps be, too, was a victim of Wilcox's and sought in an indefinite way to warn him. Perhaps he was a madman, perhaps he really was Wilcox's solicitor, bent on a peacemaking errand. Mr Kershaw could reach no conclusion, but presently the value of the advice began to dawn on him. He would call on Wilcox; he had had no intimation of the latter's murder and it would be surely an unusual thing for a murderer to go and pay a social call on his victim. It would help to mislead the police.

But no time was to be lost. At any moment his servant might burst in on him with the dreadful news; he marvelled she had not done so before.

Putting on his hat he left the house and, with as much composure as he could command, walked over to Mr Wilcox's house and rang the bell.

The butler, calm and dignified as usual, opened the door. 'Good morning, Mr Kershaw,' he said. 'Will you walk in; Mr Wilcox said you were to be shown in to him if you called.'

Mr Kershaw was staggered. What did all this mean? Wilcox was dead, he himself had killed him. He recovered himself as best he might and followed the butler. The latter threw open the library door. 'Mr Kershaw, sir,' he announced.

Mr Kershaw entered the library. Mr Wilcox, fully dressed, was sitting in front of his desk, on which lay various papers. He was deathly pale and trembling violently; his right hand lay half concealed in a partly opened drawer. As Mr Kershaw entered his hand moved, and Mr Kershaw heard a heavy metal object rattle against the side of the drawer.

'Good morning, Kershaw,' said Mr Wilcox in a low voice; and as his visitor advanced across the room towards him, 'No nearer,' he screamed. 'Sit in that chair by you. Don't come any nearer.'

He partly withdrew his hand from the drawer and Mr Kershaw saw that it held a revolver.

Mr Kershaw seated himself and there was silence. Presently Mr Wilcox began in a thin, quavering voice: 'I am glad you have called, Kershaw, very glad, I – I wanted to see you – I wanted to talk things over a bit with you. Perhaps I was a little hasty yesterday, but it was a joke, a bad joke, if you like.' He went on with a sickly smile, 'But now it is different. I am sure we can come to an agreement – I am so sorry for what happened yesterday afternoon.'

He stopped. Mr Kershaw gazed at him.

'I hardly understand you,' he said, 'Yesterday afternoon?'

'Yes, yes,' broke in the other, 'our quarrel, you know. Now we must not quarrel; we must be friends again. Look – No, don't come nearer; I'll throw you the papers; here is a copy of a letter and a telegram to my lawyers, sent off this morning to stop all proceedings; and here,' he threw over another paper, 'is a letter to you agreeing to go back to our old understanding and saying that I'll find the money you want. It is not quite in legal shape yet,' he went on, 'but it will serve, yes, it will serve till we can get a new agreement drawn.'

Mr Kershaw took up the papers and gazed dully at them.

'They seem to be all in order,' he said, 'but I don't understand. Am I mad? Are you Wilcox? Why are you sitting there? Did I dream last night?'

The other turned even more ghastly than before. 'Then did you dream it too?' he cried. 'Did you dream, as I dreamed, that you came into my bedroom last night and throttled me to death?'

In the Woods

The old woman raised herself from stooping among her vegetables, and looked upwards towards the wood topping the hill above her. Her glance was arrested by a pair of moving figures. Shading her eyes with her hand against the westering sun, the old woman gazed more attentively at them, and distinguished, outlined against the blackness of the fir-trees, the figures of a young girl and a large dog. Slowly they mounted the grassy slope, and as they drew near the wood its shadow seemed to her to stretch itself forward to meet them. They passed on, and vanished in its recesses. The old woman bent again to her task.

*   *   *

The girl was tired, tired and unhappy. She was tired with that tiredness that at seventeen seems hopeless and unending. It is a tiredness of the mind, an ill far worse than any physical fatigue. She was unhappy with an unhappiness that, being in a sense causeless, is all the more unbearable. She felt herself to be neglected, to be misunderstood. Not, be it remarked, that she was neglected in the sense in which we apply it to those in poverty and distress. On the contrary, she was doubtless, and she herself knew it, an object of envy to many. She lacked for no bodily comfort, she owned to no neglect of the mind. Governesses had implanted that which we call knowledge in her, affectionate parents had lavished their love and care upon her. She had been watched, guided, advised, taught with all possible care. She knew all this; and she knew that if she expressed a reasonable wish for any concrete thing she would promptly possess it. But yet she felt herself neglected. A lonely child, without brother or sister, and lacking the power or the will to find close friends among the other girls of her neighbourhood, she had been compelled to rely on her parents and their friends. In childhood she had been happy, but now, with the passing of the years, she felt, dimly and indistinctly perhaps, that she was isolated and alone.

She moved onwards into the recesses of the wood, the great St Bernard beside her, treading with familiar steps the well-known track, letting her eyes rest on the stately beauty of the trees and her tired thoughts draw repose from their profound calm. Her way led gradually upwards over the crest of a ridge covered with the dark grandeur of Scotch firs. In a few moments after entering the wood the trees, closing their ranks behind her, blotted out every glimpse of the valley whence she had come. In front and on each side of her they rose, towering, straight and tall, with clean stems, upwards to where their dark-green foliage branched out and almost hid the sky. Here and there rare gaps appeared, and in these open spaces the bracken leapt up to gaze upon the sun, and waved its green fronds in the gentle breeze. Her footsteps fell noiseless on the smooth dry pine-needles as she hurried on, drinking in the first feelings of rest, the rest and peace of the great woods.

Presently the trees began to thin in front of her, the gaps among them became more frequent and larger, and soon, passing out of the fir-wood, she gazed down on to a happy valley between two ridges. Beyond the valley the fir-trees recommenced, black and formidable-looking against the slowly setting sun, except away to her left, where the declining ridge opposite sank gently into more open country, and she could descry beyond the trees a fair prospect of unwooded fields. In front of her, as she emerged from among the pines, was a pool of still water, fed by a little brook, which meandered down a green and wooded valley, a valley of osiers and willow and hazel, carpeted at this season with buttercups and ragged-robin, and fringed by tall fox-gloves, by flowering elder and mountain ash. Among these lesser plants an occasional oak towered up, gnarled and misshapen, resembling, beside the stately firs, some uncouth giant of a bygone age.

The wood was very still, the afternoon hush lay upon it, there were no sounds save a gentle whispering of the wind among the fir-tops and the occasional harsh cry of a jay, startled by the rare sight of a human form, or the metallic note of a moor-hen swimming across the pool with its queer clockwork-like motion. With these sounds mingled the gentle tinkle of water escaping from the pool over a hoary flood-gate, and trickling away towards the cultivated lands below. All else was silent and moveless, and the girl, seating herself on the stump of a long-vanished tree, relapsed into absolute quiet, the dog lying equally still beside her.

The peacefulness of the scene calmed the vexed thoughts that had perplexed her; gradually the last gift of Pandora reasserted itself. She began to feel more confident in herself and in her future. True, the way was weary and long, lack of sympathy, lack of interest prevented her, but she felt that within herself lay the seeds of great deeds; the world would yet hear of her, success would yet be at her feet. Formless were the dreams, uncertain even in which direction they would be realised, but chief among them was her dream of music, her beloved music. The paths to many an ambition are closed to women, this she bitterly realised, but at any rate music lies open to them. The visions became more clearly defined, the tinkling water, the rustling pines resolved themselves into stirring rhythms and interlacing harmonies. In her excitement she moved slightly; the great dog, opening his eyes, glanced up, and licked the hand of his companion. This recalled her to herself; she looked up with a start, first at the evening sky and then at her watch, and with a little exclamation at the lateness of the hour hastened to retrace her footsteps through the trees. Presently she emerged again on the open hillside, and hurried downwards; the trees, bending to the rising wind, seemed to reach out long arms after her.

The woods enthralled her.

Her days were spent more and more dreaming in their recesses. She was much alone. Her father, a busy man, breakfasted, and was gone till evening, before she came down of a morning, an early tradition of delicate health having made her a late riser. In the evening, on his return, he was usually tired, kind but tired. Her mother, long an invalid, was away from home on an interminable cure, and in her absence even the rare visits of dull, country neighbours ceased. And so she lived, surrounded by comforts, a forgotten girl!

She grew more and more abstracted and dreamy: she neglected her duties, even her personal appearance suffered. The servants, who had long regarded her as eccentric, began to grow anxious, even a little alarmed. She became irregular in all her habits; she would stray away into the woods for hours, careless of time. In her rambles she became familiar with every corner of the woods; she was a familiar figure to the watchful gamekeeper and to the old woodman at his work. With these she was on a friendly footing. Once convinced that the great St Bernard harboured no evil intentions as regards his pheasants, the keeper was civil enough and, after a word or two of salutation, used to stand and watch the lithe, lonely, brown-clad figure slipping away from him among the brown tree trunks with a queer mixture of sympathy and bewilderment. But with the old woodman the young girl made closer friends. She loved to watch him at his solitary toil, and to note in his lined face the look of one who has lived his life in solitude among the beauties of the woods, and who has become cognisant of their glories and of part of their mysteries. She would speak to the old man but little, she spoke to few and rarely in those days, but her watch of him was sympathetic, and she seemed to be trying to draw from him something of that woodland mystery in which he was steeped.

And alone in the woods she grew ever closer to them; the trees began to be for her more than mere living trees: they began to become personalities. At first only certain of them were endowed with personality, but gradually she became aware that each tree was a living and a sentient being. She loved them all, even the distorted oak-trees were her friends. Lying prone in her favourite corner overhanging the pool, the forest become more and more alive, and the firs waving and rustling in the wind were souls lifting up their voices to God. She imagined them each with a living, separate soul, and mourned for a fallen giant as if it were a friend. Ever more and more rapt she became, more and more silent and unresponsive to her fellow-men. At times her father would gaze earnestly at the silent girl, clad in her simple white frock, seated opposite him, but he could discern nothing to disturb him. Her mother wrote, and the girl answered; letters of affection, but covering up within herself all the deep mysteries and yearnings of her heart.

The woods enthralled her.

In them, as she paced to and fro or rested on the stem of some fallen tree, listening to the rustling of the branches around, she became conscious that they were ringing with melody. She felt that here, and here alone among the trees, she could produce that divine music which her soul held expressionless within her. Vainly she would strive in her music room to reach even the lowest terrace of that musical palace whose grandest halls were freely opened to her among the solitudes of the woods.

Little by little did she become absorbed into them; she dared not as yet visit them at night, on account of the certain annoyance of her father, but by day she almost lived in them, and her belief in the souls of the trees grew stronger and ever stronger. She would sit for hours motionless, hoping, believing, that at any moment the revelation might come to her, and that she would see the Dryads dancing, and hear the pipes of Pan. But there was nothing. 'Another day of disappointment,' she would cry.

The summer passed on, one of those rare summers which only too seldom visit our English land, but which, when they do appear, by their wonderful beauty and delight, serve to make us thankful to be alive if only to enjoy the joys of Nature.

On one of these glorious days the girl had wandered out, as usual, into the woods. It was afternoon, the sky was cloudless, the wind was almost still, but at times a gentle breath from the west made a soft rustling amongst the pine branches far overhead. As the girl moved on she gazed around her on the well-known trees. All was as usual; Nature spread her beauties before her, glorious, mysterious, veiled from the ken of the human soul. The girl stopped. 'Is there nothing,' she cried, 'nothing behind this? Is Nature all a painted show? Oh, I have so longed for Nature, to find the peace, and pierce the mystery of the woods, and nothing comes in answer to my soul's call!' She moved on again, passionate, eager, yearning, with all the yearning of youth and growth for the new, the wonderful. Presently she reached her seat above the pool, and sitting down buried her face in her hands. Her shoulders heaved, her feet beat the ground in hasty emotion, her soul cried out in longing.

Suddenly she ceased to move, for a moment longer she sat in her old attitude, then, lifting her face, she gazed around her. Something had happened! Something, in those few moments! To her outward eye all was unchanged, the pool still lay silent in the sunlight, the breeze still murmured in the tree-tops, the golden-rod still nodded in the sun at the verge of the pool, and the heather still blazed on the lower slopes of the ridge opposite her. But there had come a change! – an unseen change! – and in a flash the girl understood. The woods were aware of her, the trees knew of her presence and were watching her, the very flowers and shrubs were cognisant of her! A feeling of pride, of joy, of a little fear, possessed her; she stretched out her arms, 'Oh, my beloved playmates,' she cried, 'you have come at last!'

She listened, and the gentle breeze among the pine-trees seemed to change, and she could hear its voices, nay, the very sentences of those voices, calling to each other in a language still strange to her ears, but which she felt she knew she would soon understand. She knew she was being watched, discussed, appraised, and a faint sense of disappointment stole over her. Where was the love and the beauty of Nature; these woods, were they friendly or hostile, surely such beauty could mean nothing but love? She began to grow fearful, what was going to happen next? She knew something great was coming, something awe-inspiring, something, perchance, terrible! Already she began to feel invisible, inaudible beings closing in upon her, already she began to know that slowly her strength, her will, were being drawn out of her. And for what end? Terror began to possess itself of her, when suddenly on the farther side of the pool she saw the old woodman, slowly plodding on his homeward way. The sight of the familiar figure, clad in his rough fustian clothes, bending under a new-cut faggot to which was tied the bright red handkerchief containing the old man's dinner-pail, a splash of bright colour outlined against the green verdure by the pool, was as a dash of cold water over a fainting man. She braced herself up, and watched the distant figure – as she did so, as silently, as suddenly as the mysterious door had opened, it closed again. The woods slept again, ignorant of and indifferent to the young girl.

But, that night, long after the household slept, the girl was at her window, gazing out across the valley to where the fir woods crowned the opposite hill. Long she watched them as they towered, irregular and mysterious, overhanging the grey moonlit fields and sleeping village below them. They seemed to her now to be a strong, thick wall defending the quiet valley below, and guarding it from ill, and now to be the advance guard of an enemy overhanging her peaceful village home and waiting but the word to swoop down and overwhelm it.

The woods enthralled her.

She felt herself on the point of penetrating their mystery; a glimpse had been given her, and now she hesitated and doubted, torn between many emotions. The fascination of fear possessed her, she dreaded and yet she loved the woods. For a day or two after her adventure she shunned them, but they lured her to them, and again and again she went, seeking, hoping for, dreading, what she knew must come. But her search was vain, silently and blindly the woods received her, though again and again she felt that after she had passed she was noted, she was discussed, and that her coming was watched for. The fascination and the fear grew; her food, her few duties, were all neglected; she felt, she knew, that her eyes would soon be opened.

The summer was over. September was upon the world of the woods: the bracken was turning into a thousand shades of yellows and browns, the heather was fading, the leaves of the early trees were browning, the bulrushes hung their dying heads, the flowers were nearly over; the golden-rod alone seemed to defy the changing year. The young rabbits, the fledgling birds, the young life, had all disappeared. At times one saw a lordly cock pheasant, or his more modest wife, strut across the woodland rides. Once in a while, with a loud clapping of wings, wild duck would rise from the pool; among the hazel bushes the squirrels were busy garnering their winter store, and from the distant fields the young girl, as she sat in her well-loved corner of the woods, could hear the far-off lowing of cattle. The afternoon was heavy and oppressive; a dull sensation of coming change hung over the woods, dreaming their last dreams of summer. The firs stood dark and motionless, with a faint aspect of menace in their clustering ranks; no birds were moving among them, no rabbit slipped from one patch of yellowing bracken to another. All was still as the young girl sat musing by her well-loved pool.

Suddenly she started up, listening. Far off, up the green valley, beyond where a cluster of osiers hid the bend, she seemed to hear a sound of piping. Very faint and far off it seemed; very sweet and enthralling; sweet, with a tang of bitter in the sweet, enthralling, with a touch of threatening. As she stood listening eagerly, and with the air of one who hears what he has hoped and longed and dreaded to hear, that same well-remembered sudden, subtle change passed over the woods. Once more she became aware that the trees were alive, were watching her, and this time she felt that they were closer, their presences were more akin to her than before. And it seemed to her as if everywhere, figures, light, slender, brown-clad figures, were passing to and fro, coming from, fading into, the brown trunks of the trees. She could not discern these figures clearly; as she turned to watch they faded out, but sidelong they seemed to flock and whirl in a giddy dance. Ever the sound of the piping drew nearer, bringing with it strange thoughts, over-powering sensations, sensations of growth, of life, thoughts of the earth, vague desires, unholy thoughts, sweet but deadly. As the sounds of the piping drew nearer, the vague, elusive figures danced more nimbly, they seemed to rush towards the girl, to surround her from behind, from each side, never in front, never showing clearly, always shifting, always fading. The girl felt herself changing. Wild impulses to leap into the air, to cry aloud, to sing a new strange song, to join in the wild woodland dance, possessed her. Joy filled her heart, and yet, mingling with the joy, came fear; fear, at first low-lying, bidden, but gradually gaining; a fear, a natural fear, of the secret mysteries unfolding before her. And still the piping drew nearer; it was coming, it was coming! it was coming down the quiet valley, through the oak-trees that seemed to spring to attention to greet it, as soldiers salute the coming of their King. The piping rose louder and more clear. Beautiful it was, and entrancing, but evil and menacing; the girl knew, deep in her consciousness she knew, that when it appeared, evil and beauty would come conjoined in it. Her terror and her sense of helplessness grew; it was very near now; the dancing, elusive forms were drawing closer around her, the fir woods behind her were closing against her escape. She was like a bird charmed by a serpent, her feet refused to fly, her conscious will to act. And the Terror drew ever nearer. Despairingly she looked around her, despairingly uttered a cry of helpless agony.

The great St Bernard lying at her feet, disturbed by her cry, raised himself to his haunches and looked up into her face. The movement of the dog recalled him to her thoughts; she looked down at him, into the wise old eyes that gazed up at her with love and with the calm look of the aged, the experienced, of one from whom all the illusions of Life had faded. In the peaceful, sane, loving look of the dog the girl saw safety, escape. 'Oh, Bran, save me, save me,' she cried, and clung to the old dog's neck. Slowly he arose, stretched himself, and, with the girl holding fast to his collar, turned towards the homeward path. As they moved forwards together the whirling forms seemed to fade and to recede, the menacing, clustered firs fell back, the piping changed and, harsh and discordant, resolved itself into the whistle of the rising wind, the very sky seemed to grow lighter, the air less heavy.

And so they passed through the woods together; and emerging from their still clutching shadows stood gazing across the valley darkening in the evening light, towards the gates of home, lit up by the cheerful rays of the setting sun.

*   *   *

The old woman, resting her aching back, looked up and saw the girl descending from the woods with quick light steps. 'I wish I were as young and carefree as she be,' she muttered, and stooped again among her vegetables.

The Late Earl of D.

The story which I am about to tell, whilst bearing some resemblance to a type of phenomena which have frequently formed the basis of tales both frankly fictitious or actually experienced, or believed to have been experienced, differs in one or two marked respects from this type and is, therefore, worthy of record. Mr Ellis, whose narrative I transcribe, has given a very clear and exact account of what befell him on that September evening in D. House; but, if it had been possible to ascertain whether the glass of the window had been changed during the fifteen years previous, it might have thrown still further light on how the phenomena were brought about. With this observation I give place to Mr Ellis.

*　　*　　*

I was but a young man when some thirty years ago I became the junior partner in Messrs Ransome and Ellis, Solicitors, of Lincoln's Inn Fields. The practice with which I thus became connected is an old-established one; sound, but of no very great magnitude, although we count several well-known and honoured families amongst our clients. Not the least among these was that of the Earl of D. and his family, the possessors of an ancient but not wealthy estate in the Midland Counties. At the date of my becoming a partner in Messrs Ransome and Ellis the direct family of D. was reduced to two persons. The present Earl was a man of over middle age, unmarried and permanently resident at D. House, where he occupied himself in local activities, both charitable and official, and bore a high repute among ministers of many denominations as an earnest and sincere Christian gentleman. His lordship in his earlier years had by no means merited this description, having led an extremely wild life, a life not altogether untarnished by performances of a somewhat disreputable nature. He had passed through Eton and Sandhurst and joined a crack cavalry regiment from which, after sundry escapades, he had been requested to resign. Thereafter he had lived the life of a fast man about town, existing, after the expenditure of his private fortune, on his wits, a method of gaining a livelihood which is neither easy nor honourable, nor always successful. On more than one occasion his elder brother, who at that time held the Earldom, came to his assistance, raised money and paid his debts for him, thereby encumbering somewhat seriously a not very wealthy property. However, after the sudden and singular death of the Earl, The Honble. Charles, as he then was, turned over a new leaf and settled down soberly at D. to devote the remainder of his life to the activities I have mentioned. He did not marry, and at his death the title was doomed to extinction, although the property would pass to his sister, Lady Margaret, the other surviving member of the family, or to her children as the case might be. Lady Margaret had long ago quarrelled with her brother and neither she nor her husband visited D. House.

I must now devote a few sentences to the late Earl. This gentleman had been an invalid from very early years, suffering from a form of paralysis which entirely deprived him of the use of his lower extremities. Thus confined to his bed, his *chaise longue* or his wheeled chair, his energies were perforce diverted to literary subjects and, being gifted by nature with an acute and powerful intelligence and a great love of learning, he succeeded in supporting existence not unhappily. By nature he was a kindly and happy soul; fond of such society as he could mingle in, he was popular among his neighbours and beloved by his tenants and other dependants. He read widely, wrote a little and meditated much. Owing to his malady he was necessarily much alone, but to this he was accustomed and he was well cared for by his confidential nurse-valet, a man named Sinnett.

During a certain September about fifteen years before I joined my firm, Mr Charles descended upon D. House and his brother for one of his rare visits, visits which my partner well knew usually meant further arrangements being made by Lord D. for money to settle his impecunious brother's affairs. Lord D. could not have been especially attached to his troublesome junior, who had been cast off by their only sister as a hopeless prodigal, but he had a lively sense of the family honour and stretched his resources to avert a stain being cast upon it. Mr Charles no doubt deliberately reckoned on his brother's sensitiveness in this respect. We do not know exactly what passed between the brothers during this last visit, but I gather that Lady Margaret had been recently protesting strongly against the possible injury to her children's interests that was being caused by Mr Charles's extravagance and that this protest, coupled with the growing sense that his brother's pocket was a bottomless pit, caused Lord D. to refuse to make any further payments. At any rate during the two or three days of Mr Charles's stay the relations between the brothers, which had not been cordial for years, grew extremely strained and on the last night of his life Lord D., after a violent quarrel, ordered Mr Charles to leave the house the next morning for ever.

It now becomes necessary to tell exactly what took place during this fatal evening, as testified to by Mr Charles, by Sinnett and by a footman.

According to the testimony of all three, the two brothers dined together in almost total silence, broken only by a few forced remarks made for the benefit of the servants. Sinnett, who acted as personal attendant at meal-times on Lord D., was no doubt fully aware of the quarrel, but the other servants might not have been so. After dinner Lord D. was wheeled into the library and established in his *chaise longue* and the two brothers were left alone. When the footman took in the coffee at about nine o'clock, he heard angry voices and Lord D. exclaiming, 'My patience and my purse are both exhausted. Tomorrow you go for good and all, and I'll send £100 to your lodgings to take you to Canada or to the Devil as you choose.'

Very shortly after this Mr Charles left the library and went towards the smoking-room. To reach this room he had to pass that occupied by Sinnett, and the latter swore at the inquest on Lord D's. body that Mr Charles had gone straight to this room and remained there. Sinnett further testified that at about half-past nine Lord D. had rung his bell; that he had gone in to him and found him much excited, and that Lord D. had said to him, 'I have done with Mr Charles for ever. He has worn out my patience at last and I have told him to leave the house tomorrow morning. See to it that the dog-cart is got ready for the half-past ten train.' He then added that he was feeling nervous and upset, asked Sinnett to hand him a book and said he would ring when he wished to go to bed. This he usually did at about half-past ten. Sinnett continued, that a little after ten Mr Charles had left the smoking-room and come to his room, where he had called his brother by a vile name and had said that he was being cast off for ever but that he would revenge himself by dragging the family name through the dirt and then, with more abuse of his brother and sister, had gone upstairs to his own room and shut the door. Sinnett remained in his room till nearly half-past eleven during which time he heard no sounds in the house (the servants, I should say, all slept and lived in another wing) and then, wondering at Lord D's. not summoning him, he had gone to the library. On opening the door he saw his master extended in the chaise-longue and on approaching him he realised that he was dead. He thereupon at once gave the alarm.

Mr Charles was the nearest to the scene and appeared in a few minutes in his night-clothes and was completely overcome by the sad sight. A doctor was promptly sent for, a small country practitioner, who unhesitatingly gave a certificate of heart failure, and it was only at the new Lord D.'s earnest wish that an inquiry was held, the verdict at which was Death from Natural Causes.

I have given Sinnett's story at the inquest at some length as he was really the only important witness. The new Lord D. himself testified readily enough to the fact of the quarrel with his brother, admitted that he had been in a financially desperate position and generally impressed the coroner and jury with a sense of his absolute frankness. On the actual death he could throw no light. He was in bed, though not asleep, when he heard Sinnett calling below and he rushed down to meet the frightened servants, pouring in from the other wing. The story was all complete and exact and though there were some who could not help vague suspicions of all not being right, and among them Lady Margaret was to be numbered, yet there was nothing to be done. Lord D. was not well received when he next visited London, and he left town without delay to take up his abode at D. and lead the life which I have already described and which gradually gained him the applause of many serious-minded persons, as well as a certain popularity in the County.

Such was the position of affairs at D. when one day my senior partner, Mr Ransome, who was at the moment laid up at home with the gout, sent me a letter which he had received from Lord D. asking him to go down to D. at once on some family business. I had never met Lord D. up to that time, and as the illness of my partner had thrown an unusual amount of work on me I was not over-anxious to take time from the office for a visit to D. However, Mr Ransome was anxious that I should go, partly in order to enable me to make his lordship's personal acquaintance and partly because he did not wish to refuse to accede to the wishes of a valuable client. It was accordingly arranged that I should go down to D. one afternoon, spend the evening at work and return to London the next day. This programme was duly commenced and one warm afternoon late in September found me arriving at D. House in a smart dog-cart.

The door was opened to me by a footman, and I was ushered at once into a study, where I found a middle-aged, serious-looking but handsome gentleman, who introduced himself as Lord D. His appearance was irreproachable and his manners were suave and urbane, but there was a something about him which repelled me; it was indefinable, but I had rather the feeling that here was a man who lived permanently masked. After a cup of tea and a brief chat, Lord D. expressed his regret at the shortness of my stay and suggested that, as time was of value, perhaps I would wish to begin my work now. On my expressing my assent he rose and showed the way to a large room, which I saw at a glance was the library, the room in which, it will be recollected, the late Lord D. had died. As his successor opened the door, I thought I noticed what appeared to be an almost imperceptible hesitation about crossing the threshold, but I may well have been wrong, for without apparent pause Lord D. led me across the room to an opposite door, which he proceeded to unlock, explaining as he did so that it was that of the muniment room, where were stored the papers I should need in my researches. Having shown me where to look for them, and having expressed the hope that I should find the library – which he said was not often used – comfortable to work in, Lord D. took his departure, leaving me to survey my surroundings.

The library was a long and rather low room. At one end was the fireplace, in which, despite the warm weather, a large fire was blazing. At the other end were two windows. In the centre of one side of the room was the entrance door and opposite to it that of the muniment room. A large writing-table stood between the two windows and a small round table was near the fireplace. Some chairs were scattered about and I especially noticed a chaise-longue fitted with a book holder, which had been pushed into one corner and which I guessed was the one in which the late lord had been found dead. After this survey of the room, I collected my papers, settled down, and worked quietly until the bell warned me it was time to prepare for dinner.

On going down to the drawing-room I was civilly greeted by Lord D. and we proceeded to the dining-room where I saw the butler for the first time. This man I already knew to be Sinnett, the late lord's body servant, who had been retained by the present peer as his butler. The man impressed me most unfavourably. He stood carelessly behind Lord D.'s chair, taking no active part in the service of the meal and wearing an air of ill-concealed insolence. I observed that he watched me closely and suspiciously as if in some way he felt my presence inimical to him.

After dinner and the departure of this ill-looking fellow, Lord D. and I smoked and chatted pleasantly on various subjects till about nine o'clock, when I suggested that I should go and finish my work as I was to make an early start the next day. Lord D. agreed, so, bidding him goodnight, I returned to the library.

I found the room insufferably hot; the night was warm, and the servants had piled up the fire with perfect disregard of the temperature outside. Accordingly, before beginning work, I threw open one of the windows and then settled down to my papers. I worked steadily and uninterruptedly for some time and at last, my work finished, I bundled up my documents, restored the various deeds to the muniment room and, having generally cleared up, walked over to the window and closed it, before finally leaving the room.

*   *   *

My hand was raised to fasten the catch of the window when, as I vaguely looked at the lighted room behind me reflected in its dark panes, I was startled at seeing a man walk quickly across it. The door was, I knew, shut and I had heard no sound and, when I swung quickly round to face the intruder, I found myself to be looking at a room as empty as I had believed it to be. Thinking that my eyes had played me false, I turned again to the window and was again confronted with the reflection of the man, who was now standing near the centre of the room. Again I looked behind me, to see nothing, and again I turned to the window and its reflections. I was in no sense alarmed, but I began to feel strongly that I was about to experience something unusual and uncanny, and it was with great curiosity that I gazed at the darkened glass.

I now saw that the whole appearance of the room differed from its actuality. The lamp no longer stood on the writing-table but on the little round one I have before referred to. The chaise longue was drawn out near this table and in it I saw part of the back of a recumbent figure. Close to the chair stood the man I had previously seen entering the room whom I now recognised to be Lord D. as he might have been some years before. With a shock I guessed I was probably seeing a vision of the last hours of the late Lord D. – for I took the figure in the chair to be his – and I watched with breathless interest.

The two men appeared to be engaged in a violent dispute and the younger, at any rate, to be beside himself with rage. He seemed to be threatening the almost motionless figure in the chair; who in turn I perceived to be making determined gestures of refusal. Suddenly the door opened and a third man appeared, whom I saw to be Sinnett. He did not advance into the room, but stood near the doorway, watching. The brothers, however, became aware of his presence, for the younger hastily crossed the room, caught Sinnett by the arm and began what seemed to be an appeal to him. While this was going on I saw, and the movement was curiously and firmly impressed on me, the reclining figure draw out a pencil and write a few words in the book it was holding. As it did so, Mr Charles, for so I shall call him, released his hold of Sinnett and sprang across the room towards his brother. As he advanced the latter let fall his book, a large red bound volume, nearly square, and raised his hands. Mr Charles did not hesitate. He snatched a cushion from under the sick man's head and pressed it down upon his face.

I turned with a cry of horror, but the room lay still and quiet as ever and I forced myself once more to turn back to the window. But all was over and the reflection in the glass showed no more than the peaceful room.

* * *

Dazed and sickened at what I had seen I sought my own room and lay wondering what I should do. I was determined on one thing, namely to leave the house without another sight of Lord D. or Sinnett. Therefore at the close of a weary night, I wrote a few lines to Lord D. to explain that I had finished my task and was leaving for London on the early train. Another thought then struck me. Why had the red bound book that Lord D. had been holding so impressed itself upon my mind, and had he written anything therein which would serve to bring his murderer to justice? The dawn was breaking, but no one was astir when I crept down to the library and searched eagerly for some little time for the book. Happily its distinctive shape and binding rendered my search successful. I found the book, anxiously looked it through and saw scribbled faintly and hurriedly on one of the pages the words 'C. is going to murder – ' That was all. Then I knew the vision of the night before to be real.

*   *   *

For a time I hesitated as to the course to pursue, but ultimately I decided to remove the leaf carefully and show it to Mr Ransome. On arriving in town I lost no time in seeking him out, telling him my story, and asking his advice as to what to do to obtain justice for the dead Earl. His opinion, however, chilled my enthusiasm, since he pointed out that no jury could possibly convict the present Earl on the testimony of a vision in a window pane and an unsigned and unfinished pencilled note. He agreed with me, that morally there could be no doubt of the present Earl's guilt, and rather ruefully assented to my argument that we could no longer continue to have any relations with him. It was, therefore, arranged that as soon as Mr Ransome returned to business he should write severing the connection, but Fate disposed otherwise.

Two days after my visit to D., Lord D. was flung from his dog-cart as he returned from a meeting and was instantly killed. Immediately after his death and before Lady Margaret had been able to take possession of D. House, Sinnett disappeared and was never heard of again. He took nothing at his flitting, but it was found that for years past he had been in receipt of a considerable income from Lord D's. purse.

Of course my story was never told to Lady Margaret. I took an early opportunity of replacing the extracted leaf in its place, having first carefully obliterated the words written on it, and the cause for our resignation having been removed my firm continued and still continues to act as solicitors for the family.

Mr Mortimer's Diary

The somewhat peculiar circumstances connected with the death of Mr Roger Mortimer, an antiquary of no little reputation in his day, over twenty-five years ago, although a nine days' wonder at the time, have now been forgotten. Nay, the very name and fame of Mr Mortimer himself have also passed into oblivion, save perhaps that his writings are still perused for the sake of curiosity by students of certain branches of antiquarian research.

As the last of Mr Mortimer's relatives has recently died and there remains no one to whom the publications of portions of his diary can give pain, and as those latter portions, conveying as they do certain strong impressions of unusual happenings, possess a certain interest to psychical investigators, it has been decided by the gentleman into whose possession the diary has now come to lay the latter portion of it before the world, eliminating from it as a matter of course any portions which might yet cause embarrassment to anyone.

Before touching upon the diary itself, it is necessary to recapitulate as briefly as possible the story of Mr Mortimer and of his death.

Mr Roger Mortimer was a gentleman born of well-to-do parents. He was an only child and was educated according to the usual practice of well-to-do folk; Eton and Oxford claimed him and at the latter seat of learning he became imbued with a passion for antiquarian research. After various essays, he finally settled down into specialising on Art in early Italy, and devoted himself to the study of Etruscan remains. He became gradually well known, first as a connoisseur and finally as a leading authority in this subject; he wrote several articles on it, one especially dealing with what he claimed to be a proof of certain close relationships between Etruscan and Egyptian artistic works. This essay provoked a sharp controversy which, besides moving along the lines common to most battles between scientific experts, was marked by a regular attack on Mr Mortimer by a man named Bradshaw, an assistant master at an obscure Yorkshire school. Mr Bradshaw, in a letter to the *Times*, claimed to be the real discoverer of the objects on which Mr Mortimer based his article and roundly asserted that Mr Mortimer had stolen them from him, and had also purloined from him the genesis of the ideas which he was now presenting to the world as his own. Acting, as he said, under the advice of friends, Mr Mortimer did not reply to the letter; a dignified silence, he maintained, was unquestionably the best answer to it. Mr Bradshaw was apparently unable to substantiate his accusation; he was a poor, unknown man, Mr Mortimer was wealthy and respected, and so the matter dropped. In private conversation Mr Mortimer readily admitted that he had met Mr Bradshaw accidentally when abroad, that the gentleman was, he believed, interested in antiquarian research, but that his sole connection with him had been to see that he was properly attended to during a serious attack of illness with which he had been seized during an expedition in the hills, whither he had gone unattended and where he was found lying ill in a miserable inn by Mr Mortimer. The episode was gradually forgotten and Mr Bradshaw was heard of no more.

In person, Mr Mortimer was a tall, thin, dark and rather severe-looking personage. He was a well-informed man on many subjects besides his own speciality; and, while living a somewhat quiet life, he by no means despised society, more especially of the more serious type, and was frequently seen at various social gatherings. He was not a man of many friends, in fact, it would be rash to assert that anyone was admitted to close intimacy with him, but he was popular with a large circle, and discharged his social obligations in punctilious fashion. As already said, he was a well-to-do man and inheriting a comfortable fortune he did not dissipate it. But he was no miser, he spent freely on his hobby and was liberal enough to all those connected with him. His moral character appeared to be unimpeachable, his temper was equable; he would prefer to speak and act kindly rather than the reverse, and in a general way he may be summed up as a worthy member of the body politic, who whilst inspiring no particular affection equally inspired no dislike, save in the single and unexplained case of Mr Bradshaw. He had been born of Roman Catholic parents and educated in that faith, but he had long abandoned the practice of any form of religion and was a convinced and almost militant upholder of the extreme materialistic school. Lastly it should be added that Mr Mortimer possessed no near relatives, had never married, and, at the date of his death, aged fifty-six years, was apparently free from care and in perfect bodily health.

Mr Mortimer had lived for a number of years in rooms in — Street, kept by a couple of retired domestic servants. These rooms consisted of the first floor of a good-sized house and comprised a front room, used by Mr Mortimer as his sitting-room and study, looking out on to the quiet and eminently respectable — Street, and a back room of lesser size, which formed the bedroom. The two rooms were connected by a short, private lobby, out of which opened a small cubicle, which had been fitted up as a private bath-room. Of course, in addition to this private passage the two rooms both opened on to the public staircase. Mr Mortimer had fitted up his apartments with a view to both taste and comfort; he spent much of his time at work on his researches in his sitting-room, which contained his private desk and papers and the walls of which were lined with bookshelves laden with many rare and precious volumes.

Objects of ancient and especially of Etruscan art were scattered about and several good watercolours of Italian scenes decorated the spaces on the walls not occupied by bookshelves. The bedroom was more sparely furnished, but still every reasonable article of comfort was to be found therein. The remainder of the house was like the first floor, let as apartments for single gentlemen. At the time of the events which are now being recorded, the ground floor was under lease to a Mr Andrew Scoones, an official in the Government service, the second floor, the one above Mr Mortimer, was temporarily empty, while the landlord and his wife, persons of the name of White, and the little maidservant occupied the top floor.

Mr Mortimer's life was one of great regularity. He was in the habit of being called precisely at eight in the morning by White, and then immediately repaired to his bathroom. In his absence White set out his clothes, and brought up to the bedroom a tray with the materials for Mr Mortimer's rather slender breakfast, which he partook of in his bedroom. While he was thus breakfasting and completing his toilet, the sitting-room was tidied up and made ready for the day and thither he would repair to attend to his correspondence and to read his newspaper. If he were occupied in any special research or writing he would then devote himself for a time to that, otherwise he usually proceeded to his Club, the Megatherium, where he spent a large part of his waking hours. Here he lunched, if not engaged elsewhere for that meal, and then passed the afternoon in various ways, returning to his rooms at about seven, to array himself for the evening, which was passed either in some social function or at the Club. Normally he returned to his rooms shortly after eleven and proceeded forthwith to bed. This programme was maintained on Sundays and weekdays, winter and summer, varied only by an annual excursion from London, either on a round of visits or quietly to some watering-place. No life more calm or open can be imagined; there appeared to be no room in it for secrets and certainly if Mr Mortimer possessed any they were closely guarded.

Such was the man, and such was the existence that was cut short by a mysterious tragedy on the night of July 16–17 in the year 18— . The story of this tragedy so far as it was revealed at the time now requires to be told.

The first sign of any unusual disturbance in Mr Mortimer's regular form of life was noted by a waiter at the Megatherium – one George Robbins. This man was the regular attendant on the little table in the cosy corner of the dining-room at which Mr Mortimer always sat. He appeared in the box at the Coroner's inquest and testified that on the evening of July 10th Mr Mortimer was dining alone; he appeared to be out of spirits and ate but little. Opposite to his seat at the little table was another chair, but this was unoccupied and no place was set in front of it. Towards the end of dinner, Robbins was astonished to see Mr Mortimer rise from his chair and move in what the witness described as a 'threatening kind of way', round the table towards the empty chair. Suddenly he stopped, leaned heavily against the table and appeared to be about to faint. Robbins came quickly to him and asked if he was ill. 'Only a turn, Robbins,' answered Mr Mortimer. 'Get me a glass of brandy,' Robbins brought it, and found Mr Mortimer already looking better: he drank the brandy and then said, 'Take that chair away', pointing to the vacant one, 'and never put it there again unless I have someone to dine with me.'

Robbins obeyed and the incident was closed, but the man could not help observing that from this time on till the end Mr Mortimer appeared always ill at ease and largely to have lost his appetite.

The next persons who were struck forcibly by a strange change in Mr Mortimer were Professor Rich, the well-known historian, and a certain Belgian scientist, M. Émile V. The latter had left England at the time of the inquest and did not testify, but Professor Rich, who was, perhaps, the most intimate of all Mr Mortimer's friends, stated that on the night of the 16th July Mr Mortimer had dined with himself and M. Émile V. at the Megatherium. The Professor had been out of town for some days, and found himself pained to observe how ill and nervous Mr Mortimer had become: he was in high but apparently forced spirits, drank more than was usual and kept announcing his intention of staying up all night.

'Few of us,' he cried, 'realise the beauty of dawn in the London streets. I shall stay here till the Club closes, and then I shall walk the streets till daylight comes. I'll have the police for company: perhaps you will hear of me as helping to catch a burglar. But I won't go home till morning.' And he began to sing fragments of the well-known old song.

The Professor was deeply shocked and the Belgian gentleman astonished; fortunately they were alone in the small smoking-room, or Mr Mortimer's conduct would have caused a scandal. Professor Rich began to expostulate with him, but with little success till Mr Mortimer's glance fell upon the door. He suddenly became silent and very pale, then, turning to the other gentlemen, he muttered something unintelligible and walked straight out of the room. It was then about a quarter-past eleven and he must have returned direct to his rooms without even claiming his coat and hat. The Professor could not in the least account for this sudden departure; no one had entered the little smoking-room nor had the door been opened.

The last person to see Mr Mortimer alive was Mr Andrew Scoones who, it will be remembered, occupied the apartments beneath those of Mr Mortimer. Mr Scoones had resided in the house for some little time, but he had only a passing acquaintance with Mr Mortimer, born of casual meetings on the stairs and similar accidental fore-gatherings. At this time, Mr Scoones was busy with a literary article and as his day was absorbed by his official duties he was in the habit of working at night. For a long time he had been undisturbed by Mr Mortimer, but for the past five or six days he had frequently heard that gentleman moving about his rooms at very late hours. He had not paid much attention to his neighbour's restlessness, however, until this night of July 16th, when he heard Mr Mortimer enter his apartment at about half-past eleven and forthwith begin to move about uneasily. As he listened a curious sense of there being something very wrong began to pervade him; and gradually it began to become known to his subconscious mind that something serious was amiss in Mr Mortimer's rooms. The impression grew stronger, and at last it overcame his natural shrinking from intruding on the privacy of an almost total stranger, and rising from his writing-table he proceeded upstairs.

On reaching Mr Mortimer's door he paused; inside he could hear Mr Mortimer pacing to and fro and occasionally uttering an ejaculation, the nature of which he could not hear. Finally he knocked at the door. There was a brief pause, then it was flung wide open with such violence that it crashed back against the wall behind it and Mr Mortimer appeared on the threshold. He was dressed in his evening clothes, and was very pale, but there were no signs of disorder either on his person or in the room, which was brilliantly illuminated.

For a moment the two men looked at each other in silence, then Mr Scoones, plucking up his courage, began: 'I beg your pardon, Mr Mortimer, if I have disturbed you, but I fear you are ill.'

'Ill?' said the other. 'What makes you think that?'

'I must renew my apology,' answered Mr Scoones, 'but I heard you tramping so restlessly overhead, and it is so late, that I feared there must be something the matter and I came up to see if I could be of any assistance.'

There was a longish pause, during which Mr Scoones grew more and more embarrassed, then Mr Mortimer slowly said: 'I thank you, Mr Scoones, but I am not ill; I only trust I have not disturbed your rest and I promise you I will give you no cause for further complaint.' These words were uttered deliberately in a somewhat peculiar voice and Mr Scoones, abusing himself for having placed himself in a foolish position, was about to say good night and turn away, when Mr Mortimer suddenly burst out: 'Don't go, don't go, I am in trouble, grievous trouble.'

He stopped abruptly and, turning round, stared into the brightly lighted, empty room behind him. To Mr Scoones's imagination, it appeared as if he was confronting some foe, invisible and inaudible to others.

'I will gladly help you, Mr Mortimer,' said Mr Scoones, 'to the best of my ability, if you will give me an idea as to what I can do.'

Mr Mortimer turned towards him again. 'If you would save my soul,' he cried, 'you will – ' As he spoke he staggered backwards one or two paces as if he were in the grip of a powerful enemy; he turned sharply again and stepping forward closed the door suddenly, swiftly and silently, and Mr Scoones heard the key turned in the lock.

He stood amazed. What had happened to Mr Mortimer, and why had he closed the door so abruptly? He waited a moment; all was silence within, then bending towards the door, he called: 'Mr Mortimer, Mr Mortimer.'

There was no reply, and he tried the door: as he had supposed, it was locked. Again he called: 'Mr Mortimer. Can I help you? What is the matter?'

The reply came instantly: 'There is nothing the matter. All is as it should be, but come again tomorrow.' The voice sounded choked and constrained; it differed in some fashion from Mr Mortimer's.

Again Mr Scoones tried. 'I fear you are ill, Mr Mortimer; for Heaven's sake open your door and let me in. I am sure you need help and comfort.' Mr Scoones hardly knew why he spoke the last two words, but as in a glass darkly he seemed to see a vision of a poor human soul fighting a lonely and a losing battle against the Powers of Darkness.

There was another short pause, then Mr Mortimer's voice rang out clear and unmistakable on the horrified ears of his listener: 'In the name of the Devil, whose servant I am, cease to annoy me. Tomorrow you shall know all.'

Mr Scoones, filled with horror and amazement, turned away and descended to his rooms, where he sat up awhile listening, but no further sounds were heard from Mr Mortimer's floor; and at last, tired out, he retired to bed to be awakened next morning by White with the ghastly news of Mr Mortimer's death.

As usual, White proceeded to Mr Mortimer's room at eight o'clock on the morning of July 17th. He knocked at the bedroom door, entered, and was surprised to find the bed empty and evidently unused, and to observe that all the lights in the room were fully turned on. Otherwise there was no sign of anything unusual except that the door into the little private lobby was open. Turning in that direction, White perceived that the light in the lobby was also burning, as well as that in the bathroom. He passed through into the sitting-room. Here at first all appeared to be in its usual condition, save that the room was brightly illuminated, but glancing towards the door White perceived Mr Mortimer lying on the floor closely huddled up against it. He hurried over to him, and looking at him saw that his own hands were closely clenched about his throat and that he was dead. White endeavoured to raise him and to unclasp the gripping fingers, but found his clutch too firm to be relaxed. He at once rushed out to give the alarm, but even in his agitation noticed that the sitting-room door was locked, an unheard-of thing, and that the key was on the inside. A doctor was summoned, and messengers to call the police and Dr Bessford, Mr Mortimer's usual medical attendant, were also despatched. By the time the latter arrived Mr Mortimer's body had been raised from the floor and laid upon a sofa, but the doctor first summoned had not yet succeeded in removing the hands from the throat. In the presence of the police Dr Bessford and his brother practitioner ultimately succeeded in releasing the deadly grip, and a hasty examination was made which disclosed the undoubted cause of death as self strangulation; the post-mortem later on showed that there was no bodily infirmity, nor any cause of death save this one alone. Both medical men testified to their amazement at so singular and so determined a form of suicide, and both, but especially Dr Bessford, as well as White, commented on the peculiar look of abject terror on the dead face. There was no evidence found of any struggle or disturbance in the room, and Mr Mortimer's clothing was quite in order. The coroner's jury brought in a verdict of Suicide in the usual form; Mr Mortimer's body was in due course buried; and the whole affair gradually passed into the limbo of forgetfulness.

Mr Mortimer left no will or any instructions, and as his next of kin and heir, a distant sailor cousin, was then absent with his ship on the China station, Mr Mortimer's solicitor took charge his of effects and affairs. The rooms in — Street were given up, the furniture sold, and the books and manuscripts packed up and stored. On returning home, Lieutenant Mortimer did not trouble himself with unpacking the latter, and it is only since his death that they have again seen the light, and that the diary has become accessible.

It was apparently Mr Mortimer's practice to keep a diary, but seemingly only spasmodically – at any rate, only fragments have been found. Unluckily there are no existing volumes of the date at which he was brought into touch with Mr Bradshaw, so there is no clue to the real relations between the two men. The diary after a long interval had been recommenced about six months before Mr Mortimer's death, but it is only of interest for the present purpose during the last eight days of his life. With this preamble the diary may now be quoted in full.

July 8th. 'I was the subject today of a singular hallucination: I believe the spiritualist jargon describes it as clair-audience. I was in my rooms dressing to dine out with Lady L. when I distinctly heard the voice of James Bradshaw saying, 'The day of reckoning will come soon.' The impression was so strong that for a moment I supposed the man to have obtained admittance to my rooms, and to be speaking to me, but on looking round I perceived I was alone. There was no one in the sitting-room, and White, for whom I rang, assured me that he had admitted no one to see me. I am of the opinion that my subconscious memory has played me a trick and has recalled to my conscious self the last words that Bradshaw spoke as he flung himself out of the room at York, after refusing my offer of £1000. It is curious that this memory should have been revived after so many years, and even more curious that it should have been revived wrongly, for I am certain that the actual words Bradshaw used were, 'The day of reckoning will come some time.' However, it is useless to speculate on these tricks of the memory.

July 9th. I have been feeling uneasy and depressed today. I cannot describe myself as ill, but I suppose I have been working too hard at my article for Robertson, and that the heat has helped to affect me; I will get away for a breath of sea air as soon as possible. It must be my physical condition acting on my mind, but I cannot get Bradshaw out of my head. I know that he considers that I did him a great wrong, but after all £1000 to a man of his means is certainly more valuable than a little notoriety or, as he would call it, fame. Besides, I greatly question if he, a totally unknown man, could ever have got his, shall I call it, discovery recognised by people of standing; it was far too revolutionary, and needed someone recognised as an authority to bring it forward. At the time of the York interview he failed to notice this point, any more than he would agree that, if I had not come to his help in Fialo and seen him through his illness, he would probably have died and his secret have died with him and been lost to the world. He is a most unreasonable fellow, and a mischief maker; I think I came well out of my encounter with him.

July 10th. On picking up *Times* this morning, I noticed in the obituary column the death of James Bradshaw, assistant master at — School in Yorkshire. He died on the eighth, so there goes Bradshaw into nothingness. For a moment I confess to a slight feeling of regret for the man, but it passed quickly; he was an enemy of mine, though an impotent one, and it is better that he should have gone. While I fail to see how he could have done me harm while alive, yet it is certain he can do me none now that he is dead.

A most extraordinary and rather perturbing hallucination occurred this evening. I was dining alone at my usual table at the Club, and had nearly finished dinner, when, looking up, I saw James Bradshaw sitting in the chair directly opposite to my seat. He was plainly discernible as he sat quite motionless gazing at me with a diabolical grin and, save that he looked several years older, he was exactly as when I last saw him at York. I looked at him for a minute, then impelled by a sudden emotion and forgetful of the *Times* notice I rose from my chair, and moved round towards him. He did not stir until I was close upon him, and then – he simply was not there. I leaned against the table feeling sick and faint and when the waiter came to my side I sent for some brandy. This revived me, but I have told the man never to leave an empty chair opposite me again. The vision was so clear, and the appearance of the figure so menacing, that I feel unnerved. I know it is hallucination, imagination, nonsense; and yet –

July 11th. My mind must be seriously affected. I slept badly last night, and woke unrefreshed; I have had dreams but I cannot recall them, but all this is nothing to the trouble that has begun to pursue me in my waking hours. James Bradshaw is here in my rooms, he follows me to my Club, he goes with me wherever I go, whether alone or with others. I cannot see him, but I know that he is here, and I constantly hear his voice. He taunts me with what happened at Fialo years ago, something that none but he and I know; he threatens me, he laughs at me. I know that it must be hallucination, but it is horribly vivid. I know that Bradshaw's body is rotting in the earth, and his spirit dissolved into nothingness, what is it then that tortures me in his form? I have been so maddened that I have answered him back, or is it answering myself back? I do not know; I can only cling to the belief that it is some bodily derangement. Dr Bessford returns from his holiday tomorrow, and I will seek help from him. I can go to no stranger. It is now past one o'clock in the morning, and I have been walking to and fro, and wrestling with James Bradshaw for hours. I must rest, I must rest, but sleep, oh, my dreams will murder sleep!

July 12th. After a hideous night, I went early to see Dr Bessford. He tells me after careful examination that physically he can find nothing wrong with me, but that mentally I appear to be over-stimulated. I must rest. What farcical nonsense! While he was actually saying the words, Bradshaw was whispering in my ear: 'Your soul is given to me.' What shall I do? What can I do? Bessford has given me a sleeping draught; I will try and see if this will not give me at least one night of immunity from my persecutor.

July 13th. How have I lived through the night, how can I live through the day, how can I continue to exist? Last night, I took my sleeping draught and forthwith my body was steeped in sleep, but my spirit, released from its earthly casing, became the sport of the powers of evil. For what seemed ages I fled through vast, grey, misty spaces, hounded ever by James Bradshaw. Wildly I endeavoured to hide, for I knew whither he was driving me. At last he seized me and dragged me onwards and now I know there is a Hell, for I have seen it, mine own eyes have seen it; for an instant, for an eternity, James Bradshaw swung me suspended over the Pit, and then with a yell of laughter he freed me, and I woke. I woke in the pale light of early morning to see Bradshaw's form by my bed-side. I stared at the figure, which stood distinct in the early light, motionless, but with threatening arm upraised, and then I heard its voice, clear but sounding as if from far, far away: 'In four days you shall be mine for ever.' It vanished, and I have lived through another day, too crushed and hopeless to think.

July 14th. Last night I passed free of disturbance, and I have felt less sensible of the hideous presence. Perhaps I can yet escape; perhaps there is yet mercy for me. For have I been so evil a man that I deserve such a doom as Bradshaw threatens? I know I have my faults, I know I have done things that cause me shame, but is there no repentance? Is there really a God of mercy to appeal to? Surely there must be, surely that Hell, which I have myself seen, is not the doom of all mankind. What shall I do? I will make amends to any I have wronged in the past; I will try and lead a better life in the future. First, I will write openly and fully and make public the whole truth of my dealings with James Bradshaw, and if he has a family I will seek them out, and make what reparation is possible and humble myself before them. Then there is that affair of Campion; he at any rate is alive, and I can straighten out matters there; and there is Ellen; she, poor, loving soul shall have justice. But I must have time to do these things, although I will not delay in commencing them; for I must not die till my tasks are all accomplished. To begin with I must sleep; Bessford's draught gave me an experience I dare not repeat, so I will get a small bottle of opium – that will give me sound sleep.

July 15th. The opium worked well enough and I slept soundly, but I woke in an agony of fear with the voice of Bradshaw resounding through my room: 'You have two days left.' I sprang out of bed and called out something, I cannot say what, some prayer, some appeal. My answer was a mocking laugh dying away in the distance. I shall go mad. I must have time to repent in, I cannot, I will not, I dare not die yet. But how can I help myself? I have forgotten how to pray. I have denied and forsaken my God for so long that now He has forsaken me. Can no one help me? Yes, there is Father Bertram to whom my dear dead mother used to go in trouble. Can he and will he help me? I can but try.

*   *   *

The powers of Hell have prevailed; I am a lost soul with none but myself to help me. In accordance with my resolve I set forth to visit Father Bertram, and was fortunate enough to find him at home. He greeted me civilly but coldly – no wonder, renegade that I am. But when I began to try and tell my story my tongue was tied, I *could* not tell my tale, for incessantly James Bradshaw was whispering in my ear, whispering words of blasphemy and despair. I stammered out some inanities and fled the house, Bradshaw walking by me laughing gleefully.

July 16th. I woke once more from a drugged sleep to hear the voice of doom proclaiming: 'Tomorrow I will claim you.' But he *shall* not do so, I will not die, I dare God or Devil to take my life till I have accomplished my purpose. Let me think calmly; I am under a spell now, a spell which tells me I must die tomorrow. Let me break that spell; let me but survive over tomorrow, and the power of evil will be defeated. I have but to preserve my will power for one day, and I am safe. I will seek outside help, the help of man, it is the night I dread. Well, I will keep in the company of my kind all night, they will preserve me from sell-destruction. I will remain at the Club as late as possible, dining with Rich and that Belgian friend of his, as he has asked me to do, then I will go out into the streets and find some friendly constable, who will let me be his companion through the night watches: but nothing shall induce me to spend the night in my rooms. In the morning I shall be safe.

The day so far has been quiet and undisturbed, if I can get through the night as I propose, I feel I shall have conquered in the fight. Alone I shall have done it: God has deserted me, the Devil assails me, but I defy them both; I will not die tonight.'

These are the closing words of the diary. It will be remembered that the unfortunate man returned from the Club to his apartments at about half-past eleven that evening.

The House in the Wood

'I do not feel called upon to vouch for the truth of the story I am going to tell you,' said the 'drummer', in whose company I was making the journey from Chicago to New York, 'I will merely say that my friend Larrabee was a man on whose word I implicitly relied, and as he told me the story several times, never contradicted himself, and always declared he was telling the truth, I, for one, believe it.'

This declaration was made by Chas Smithson, a commercial traveller for the large New York importing house of Higsby and Dayland, in the smoking-room of the vestibuled limited express from Chicago to New York, one fine April morning not a hundred years ago. I knew Mr Smithson slightly, and knew him to be as good a fellow as ever breathed, and when I had entered the train at Chicago the night before I had been heartily glad to see his jovial self preceding me. We had assembled in the smoking-car of the train, a party of half a dozen, the usual kind of gathering one sees on such a trip. After the various staples of conversation had been discussed and dismissed, there had been somewhat of a break in the conversation, interrupted by someone enquiring: 'Does anyone here believe in ghosts?' This remark had occasioned the wrangle always incident upon it; and story after story, some old, some new, had been narrated, and canvassed, and the anti-ghost party had gradually but slowly been winning the day, when Smithson, who had hitherto, unlike his usual self, been silent, suddenly made the above observation. There was a dead silence. Smithson had spoken with such unusual vehemence that everyone saw that, mild though the words of his speech were, yet underlying their mildness was an evident deep-rooted meaning that the subject was a grave one, and should not lightly be discussed. We all turned towards him, and in one voice demanded that he should tell his tale.

After a moment's pause he said: 'Well, gentlemen, I will do so, but I request that none of you will laugh at me. My friend, Mr Larrabee, who is lately dead, was an eye-witness, or at least believed himself to have been an eye-witness, of what I am going to relate; and firmly believed as I do that he witnessed a spiritual manifestation take place with a view to accomplishing a definite object. Though the adventure did not happen to myself,' he added, 'I will by your leave tell it in the first person, as I think I can thus do it better justice.'

So after another round of drinks had been ordered and disposed of, and all the cigars had been properly lighted, we settled ourselves in our chairs, and prepared to listen in the prosaic smoking-room of the limited express to one of the most astonishing stories we had ever heard solemnly told as true.

'Some years ago,' commenced Smithson, in the character of Larrabee, 'it happened to be my fate to be a travelling salesman for a big Boston house, which had a branch in Chicago, and my route led me into the northern part of Wisconsin and into Minnesota; and, in fact, embraced that part of the country where many of the great iron mines are situated. The country was then much wilder than it is now, railroad transportation was poor, and justice and the enforcement of the law also were very negligently attended to. The journeys, too, were over rough and unfrequented roads in many instances, while the hotel accommodations were always bad. However, I was quite young then and, as my sales were good, I did not particularly mind the hardship of the life.

'I remember that the hardest part of the task allotted to me and the part I was always most glad to have done with was my visit to the village of Milnaska, which lay some thirty miles from the end of a little branch railroad connecting with the main line for Chicago. My custom was to put up for the night at the railway terminus, spend the next day in a buggy driving through the hilly, forest-covered country to Milnaska, sleep there, spend the next day, and then early in the following morning return in time to catch the evening train to the South. Milnaska was, though off the line of travel, a place of sufficient importance to make this trip desirable, especially lately, since an iron mine of some consequence had been opened in its immediate vicinity.

'The road from the railroad terminus to Milnaska was one of the most dreary I have ever seen; for Milnaska being close to the shore of Lake Superior its iron was sent off by boat, and most of its supplies received in the same way, so that there was very little travel between it and Little Forks, as the railroad terminus was named. Though the Lake was the easiest way of getting to Milnaska, it was not the quickest either from Chicago, where the headquarters of the mining company were, or for myself, who came to Milnaska from a point further west.

'One dreary October evening in the year of Our Lord 18— beheld me tired and dirty, disembarking from the train at Little Forks, and seeking the seclusion of the one uncomfortable and not particularly clean hotel the place boasted. On my arrival at its inhospitable doors, I registered, and having no business in Little Forks, and no desire to wander about its uninviting streets, I quietly sat down by the stove to await the announcement of supper. A few of the usual country hotel loafers were grouped about the hotel office, but there was no one who excited my particular curiosity, till there entered a gentleman whom, travel learned as I was, I had great difficulty in "placing". A native of Little Forks he certainly was not, but that he knew the place was equally certain, and that he was known in it, for the landlord hastily advanced to greet him, calling him Mr Sykes, and shaking him by the hand. But he certainly was not a drummer, or the landlord would have offered to take the little unpretentious black bag he carried, and this he did not do. The stranger walked up to the desk and, still resting his left hand on his bag, registered, whilst the landlord observed, "The fast buggy at eight tomorrow morning as usual, Mr Sykes?" To which the other responded only by a nod, and preceded by the bell boy disappeared up the stairs. I ought, I suppose, to give a short description of Mr Sykes, and a short one will do, for he was one of those negative men, who have no very marked character- istics. Rather short and squarely built, his grey hair and lined face rather marked the man who had suffered than the old man. But though his countenance bore signs of sorrow, yet it showed also courage and great resolution, coupled with keen watchfulness. He was dressed in deep black, evidently in remembrance of some lately-lost loved one.

'As soon as Mr Sykes had disappeared, I strolled over to the desk, and after a few remarks I asked the landlord who Mr Sykes was. The man looked queerly at me for a few moments, and then said, "I am sorry, Mr Larrabee, you can see for yourself in the register that he comes from Chicago, but I am not able to tell you anything about him. Mr Sykes is very particular, and has requested me never to mention who he is, or what is his business. But," he continued, "to oblige you as a good customer, I'll put you at the same table at supper, and you can get what you can out of him. But he is awful close-mouthed. I'll tell you this, though, he is going to Milnaska tomorrow."

'I was obliged to be content with this answer and wait till supper time, which luckily was not far off. As soon as it was announced I walked in, and seating myself had got about a quarter of the way through my very leathery beefsteak, when the landord, true to his promise, ushered Mr Sykes to the seat next mine. He ordered supper, and while it was being brought sat quietly looking around him. I was surprised to see that he had brought his black bag down with him, and that it lay on the chair next him. Presently I decided to break the ice, and did so with the remark, "Bad weather, isn't it?" "Yes," replied Mr Sykes. "I am mighty sorry I have got to drive to Milnaska tomorrow," I went on. "if it goes on raining like this, I shall be wet through in half an hour." "Indeed," answered my neighbour.

'This taciturnity irritated me; I was determined to find out some-thing about him, so after a moment's pause I said, "If it isn't taking a liberty, sir, may I ask if you are going to Milnaska too?" He shot a quick, suspicious glance at me, then slowly answered, "Yes, I am." "Well," said I, "in that case, what do you think of our going over together? It is a dull trip at best. I have made it often enough to know. My name," I continued, "is Larrabee. I represent Potter and Dennis of Boston. What name did you say yours was, sir?" "My name is Sykes," he replied, "I am in the employ of the Milnaska Mining Co. of Chicago."

'He gradually became somewhat more friendly, possibly under the influence of the supper, and when we went out into the hotel office I saw him walk up to the landlord and exchange a few words with him, evidently about myself, from the looks they cast in my direction. Mr Sykes then joined me near the stove, still clasping his precious bag, and talked for some little time pleasantly and well. By the time for retiring, we had agreed to make the trip to Milnaska and back together, as we discovered that we should neither of us have to spend more than one day there. We went to rest early agreeing to start at eight o'clock the following day.

'The next morning broke raw and damp, and after breakfast, when Mr Sykes and I went outside to look at the roads, we saw that we should have a bad trip of it and be lucky to get through without mishap. However, we had got to go, and as we both knew the road, and the landlord knew he could trust us, we decided not to overload the buggy with a driver, but be our own charioteers. We started cheerfully enough, Mr Sykes having first carefully lashed his black bag under the seat with a stout bit of cord, and for some little time proceeded slowly along chatting pleasantly. We had taken a light lunch with us, there being no hotel on the road. We drove along for a considerable time, and having become absorbed in an energetic political discussion we did not notice what slow progress we were making. Presently, however, we awoke to the fact that at the rate we were now going we should not reach Milnaska that night and accordingly quickened our pace. But the roads were in a fearful condition and though we had been promised a good horse only a sorry jade had actually been put between the shafts.

'We both worked, however, and worked the harder, as the rain was again beginning to fall and the wind to rise and blow in our faces, thus still further retarding our progress. Still we managed to proceed and, though I think it would have been late, yet we should have reached Milnaska that night, had not our unfortunate horse suddenly gone dead lame. Here was a predicament! We were we scarcely knew how many miles from either Little Forks or Milnaska, in the heart of the pine woods, with a broken-down horse, and night, accompanied by a violent storm, rapidly coming on.

'After gloomily cogitating over the situation I suddenly remembered that about two-thirds of the way between Little Forks and Milnaska was an old, rambling frame house, tenanted apparently by some squatter's family. I recollected that we had not yet passed it and, judging by the distance we had travelled that it could not be very far off, I suggested to Mr Sykes that we should make the best of our way there on foot, leading the horse, seek shelter for the night, and either borrow a new horse in the morning or try to reach Milnaska with our present steed. "I had already thought of the Joneses' place," said Mr Sykes in reply, "but I don't like it, I don't want to go there." "Why not?" said I. "It seems to be the only place there is?" "Well, I suppose we must try it," replied Mr Sykes.

'We pushed on through the pouring rain and driving wind for about a mile, when at a turn in the road to my great joy I saw a light gleaming through the gathering darkness, and in a few moments we reached the door of an old-fashioned frame house. The house which we drew up before stood end on, as I afterwards discovered, to the road. It was an old, two-storey log house, of great solidity of construction, possibly having been built to resist marauding Indians, though its peculiar situation, backed up against the side of a hill, seemed to render this doubtful. At first sight it appeared much smaller than it really was, owing to its position and to the entrance being at one end. A rough, unkempt garden ran back from the road, and at one end of this were a barn and a storehouse in a very tumble-down condition.

'As soon as we drew up at the door, there appeared from within a tall, slatternly looking woman, who stood on the threshold eyeing us in silence. I addressed her as politely as I could, asking her if we could have a night's lodging for man and beast. For a moment she made no reply, then sullenly said, "No, you can't." I was so surprised at this lack of politeness that I remained speechless till presently, roused by the voices he had heard, a gaunt, powerful-looking man came up from behind the woman and stared out at us. To him I addressed myself, again asking for lodging, explaining our predicament and offering to pay well for a night's entertainment. At first he, too, seemed inclined to refuse, when suddenly catching sight of Mr Sykes's face behind the top of the buggy he said, "Well, I guess you can; Jenny," turning to the woman, "we ain't the folk to turn travellers from the door. Come in, come in, you are welcome.' So saying he came out into the rain, helped us to alight and, ordering his wife to show us the way into the house, led off our horse towards the barn.

'We followed the woman into the low, dirty kitchen into which the door opened and, Mr Sykes still retaining his precious bag, sat down by the fire to dry and get warm. There was nothing remarkable in the aspect of the kitchen. It was perhaps rather dirtier than most and there was a lack of the comforts and bright, pretty things frequently seen in farmers' houses. I judged that Jones must spend most of his time hunting by the various sportsman's accoutrements in the room, and while I was still speculating on the delights of a hunter's existence he himself entered. "Well," said he, "I have fixed up your horse, he'll be all right in the morning, I guess he found these roads powerful heavy to draw you two fellows over. Are ye going to Milnaska, Mr Sykes?" he added. "Yes," replied Mr Sykes. "Usual business I suppose this time of the month, ain't it?" continued Mr Jones with a grin. "There's some folk will be mighty glad to see you to Milnaska, I reckon."

'My companion made no reply, and our host turned to me. We quickly found a congenial subject in the shape of fishing, and I had begun to lose the instinctive dislike I had taken to the man in the discussion of a favourite topic, when we were summoned to supper by Mrs Jones. We seated ourselves at the table and were soon busy in the discussion of a plain though very welcome repast. Once during the meal my suspicions of my host were roused from the sleep into which the fishing discussion had lulled them by noticing a queer look pass between him and his wife, as they saw Mr Sykes place his black bag under his chair.

'At the end of the meal Jones said, "I suppose, gentlemen, you are kinder cold after the rain, what do you think of a drop of the best stuff in Wisconsin?" I had no objection, and our host rose and went to a rather dark corner of the room, where he commenced fumbling in a cupboard containing quite a number of bottles. I watched and saw him take down three glasses and a demijohn of whisky. At that moment Mrs Jones dropped a plate with a a a crash; I turned to look and, as I turned towards my host again, saw him coming back with the three glasses of whisky in his hand. We each took one, and I, after carefully tasting mine and finding it, as Jones had promised, excellent, drank it down. So did Mr Sykes, and as he set down his glass once more I noticed a peculiar look pass over our host's face.

'We sat for some little time gossiping after this, and presently Mr Sykes, who had rapidly been becoming drowsy, announced his desire to retire. I said I would go too, and Mr Jones preceded us up the narrow stairway to the upper hall. On arriving at the top of the steps for the first time I became aware of how large the house was. The stairs ran up at one end of it, and opened into a passage which led back quite a distance. I was given little time to speak to Sykes. Mrs Jones had come up with us and, addressing me, she said, "Come this way to your room." I followed her down the whole length of the passage, having a vague consciousness that Jones had escorted Mr Sykes and his black bag into a room near the staircase, and was shown into a large, poorly furnished room at the end of the hallway. Bidding me good night in a harsh voice, Mrs Jones set down the lamp and departed.

'My room, as I have said, was large and ill furnished. There was a repulsive-looking bed in the centre, a chair, a little table supporting a water basin and jug, and two pocket-handkerchief towels and an old wardrobe. The room smelt close, and my first move was to the window. It was with a sense of relief I threw it open and looked out. The rain had ceased, and the full moon shone brightly on the pine woods, which lay ghostly still. Right from under my window the ground sloped sharply upward, and I experienced a queer feeling of pleasure when I noticed that it was within easy jumping distance of my window. After a few minutes, being very sleepy, I cast off coat, waistcoat and shoes, and having fastened the door as best I could I threw myself on the bed and was soon sound asleep.

'I awoke with a start, and with the impression firmly fixed on my mind that someone was calling me. I lay with my face to the open window, through which the moon was still streaming, making all within the room as light as day. I lay for an instant straining my ears, when again, this time unmistakably, and close to me, the voice, sounded. "Mr Larrabee," it said, "Mr Larrabee, get up, get up quick." The voice was faint and low; it appeared to be that of a girl, and to sound from behind me. I turned quickly, and saw standing close to my bed, and near enough for me to touch, the figure of a girl of about twelve. She was neatly and prettily dressed, and her face, as I could make out distinctly in the moonlight, was refined and gentle. Even at the time I know I thought it strange that the moonlight should be so bright as to enable me to make out her dark blue eyes and golden-coloured hair, but I could distinguish them plainly.

'I remained lost in wonderment as to who my visitor was and how she had got in to me. I knew I had locked the door, and the window was full high for her to get in at. Besides, who was she, and why had I not seen her at supper-time? She was surely too dainty a child to be the daughter of the Joneses.

'Whilst I still lay wondering, she spoke again. "Come, Mr Larrabee, Father's in danger, follow me, quick, quick, quick." There was an air of authority about her that compelled obedience, so slipping out of bed I followed her. I remember stopping to unlock my door as I went through, and noticing that no sound of steps or rustle of garments accompanied my guide's progress.

'But as we stole softly down the passage, my attention was attracted by a faint light in Sykes's room. I hastened forward, thinking something was wrong, lost sight of the girl, and pushed open the door of the room. As I entered and gazed round I saw by the faint light of a lamp Mr Sykes stretched on the bed, apparently in a drugged sleep, and Jones bending over him, whilst Mrs Jones was endeavouring to force open the black bag with a knife. They gave a cry of amazement as they saw me enter, and for a moment stood paralysed; then Jones, leaving the bedside, came forward. "I heard the gentleman cry out," said he, "Mrs Jones and I thought he was sick, and came up to do what we could for him. He is mortal bad, I am thinking."

'Taking no notice of this remark, I walked up to the bed, and ordering the discomfited couple to put down the bag, which Mrs Jones said she was trying to open to see if it contained medicine, and to leave the room, I pushed Mr Sykes by the shoulder, and after some trouble succeeded in arousing him from his drugged sleep. He started violently when he came to his senses and, recognising me, eagerly asked for his bag. I showed it to him, and having examined it and found it unopened he asked how I came to be there. I told him of my mysterious visitor, and of the intruders I had expelled from his room, and then for the first time I began to wonder where the girl was. She had disappeared, and I was anxious to find her, to take her away with us in the morning out of reach of the Joneses' vengeance. "What was she like?" asked Mr Sykes. "I have never heard of anyone living in this house except the Joneses."

'I told him that she was golden-haired with dark blue eyes. He seemed strangely agitated. "What were the words she used?" he said. "Why," I answered, "they were, 'Come, Mr Larrabee, Father's in danger, follow me quick, quick, quick.'" "My God," he exclaimed, "can this be so? Mr Larrabee," he went on earnestly, "just before you roused me, I was dreaming that my little daughter, my own little Maud, who died six months ago, was standing calling to me to wake up. I tried to do so, I struggled, for I could hear her plaintive little voice, but a weight oppressed me and I could not. It is the hand of God," he said solemnly; and bowing his head became absorbed in prayer or meditation. I left the room, but established myself outside, where I remained on guard for the rest of the night. Early the next morning Mr Sykes joined me. "Let us leave this house," he said, "as quickly as may be."

'We went downstairs, but found no one. Apparently the Joneses had fled in fear of us, and so, making the best meal we could out of the scraps in the larder, we went out to the barn and, harnessing up our horse, were soon once more on our way to Milnaska. On the road Mr Sykes informed me that he was the paymaster of the Mining Company in Milnaska, and once a month had to convey a quantity of money to that place to pay the men employed there. He was well-known on the road, but had never been molested, though he had never before tried the experiment of putting up for a night at Jones's place. The latter had a bad character, and I heard afterwards that this last episode caused him finally to decamp from the vicinity with his wife. We met with no further adventure, and arrived in Milnaska in due course, where I parted from Mr Sykes, not without the assurance of seeing him again whenever I might be in Chicago.'

'That is the story of my late friend, Mr Larrabee,' said Mr Smithson. 'I believe him to have been a truthful man, and I consequently for one believe in ghosts.'

This dogma we none of us felt inclined to dispute, especially as the welcome call, 'Dinner now ready in the dining-car', was heard approaching.

The Steps

The following story purports to be the actual experience of one of our leading medical men, who, during the late war, attained considerable eminence in the treatment of nervous diseases and affections of the brain. The earlier part of the tale has been collected from other sources for the purpose of bringing about the necessary explanations of the experience itself.

At the beginning of the war, Sir Arthur H. was living with his wife and only unmarried daughter at their place in Hampshire. Sir Arthur was a soldier, and soon after the outbreak of hostilities was despatched to a command Overseas, leaving Lady and Miss H. in charge of Atherfield Court, which is situated in an accessible and pleasant part of Hampshire. The advantages of the neighbourhood caused it to be selected by the War Office as the site for an instructional camp for the new Army, and the quiet lanes around Atherfield were soon alive with khaki-clad men, exotic-looking mules and motor vehicles of every type and size. Lady and Miss H. were both of them anxious to take their place in giving pleasure to our young soldiers, and besides occasional entertainments for the men, they threw open the doors of the Court to the officers of their acquaintance, who were cordially invited to bring their friends with them.

Among the officers so brought was a certain Captain X., a man slightly older than most of the officers of his rank and an agreeable, cultivated and travelled man. He was very popular in his Mess and had the reputation of being a capable officer, but no one knew much about him. Like so many other of the men who came to the aid of the old country from Overseas, he had no friends in England and if he had family ties here he never spoke of them.

At first he was very much liked by both Lady and Miss H., and was a very welcome visitor; but after a time the two ladies reached the conclusion that, charming and well-educated as he was, he lacked that indescribable something which characterises a gentleman. However, they did not vary their hospitality towards him on that account, and he became gradually one of their most frequent visitors.

This state of things was interrupted after a time by Captain X. proposing marriage to Miss H., a proposal which she promptly and emphatically declined. Thereupon he ceased for a while to visit the Court, but after a certain interval once more reappeared there and gradually resumed his old habit of frequent visits. The ladies did not greatly like this, and endeavoured by a colder manner towards him to discourage any intimacy; and matters remained on this slightly strained footing until Lady H. learned that the battalion to which Captain X. was attached, having completed its training, was about to proceed to France.

A few days before it left Captain X. called, ostensibly to make his farewells, but to the surprise and annoyance of Miss H. he seized an opportunity and once more offered himself as a suitor for her hand. She repulsed him firmly and finally, and a somewhat unpleasant scene took place, Captain X. vowing that come what might he intended to marry her and that, though she might refuse him now, a time would come when he would carry his point. Naturally angered, Miss H. replied equally emphatically that no earthly power would force her to marry him, and the two parted on very strained terms. A few days later the battalion went abroad, nothing further having been heard at Atherfield of Captain X., and in fact nothing more was heard from him.

For some little time various officers of the battalion who had been entertained by the H.'s kept up a desultory correspondence with them, and very occasionally one or other of them mentioned Captain X.'s name, but he himself neither wrote nor sent any message to Atherfield, and gradually the memory of him became dim, to Lady H. at any rate. Miss H., if indeed she ever thought of him, never spoke of him, and the whole episode of his acquaintance seemed in a fair way to be forgotten.

About a year later Lady H. and her daughter were sitting in the drawing-room at Atherfield, the former busily writing letters for the afternoon post and the latter immersed in a book. Both were silent and deeply intent on their respective occupations. Suddenly Miss H. started and, laying down her book, exclaimed: 'Who can that be coming down the passage?' adding after a moment's pause, 'It sounds like that horrid Captain X.'s footsteps.'

Lady H., who had heard nothing, looked up from her letters, saying placidly: 'That is quite impossible, my dear, and I do not think there is anybody in the passage, at least I hear no one.'

Miss H. listened for a moment or so longer and then said: 'No, I was mistaken, but I certainly thought I heard someone walking quickly and rather uncertainly along the passage, and for a second the idea that it was Captain X. came into my head. I cannot think why I should have thought it was him, I fancied I had forgotten him. Anyway,' she went on, 'I was quite wrong because evidently there was nobody at all and I must have been dreaming.'

Saying this, she picked up her book and Lady H. resumed her letters and thought no more about the occurrence.

Two days later Lady H. when looking through the list of Killed in Action in *The Times* noticed the name of Captain X. She did not associate this event in any way with the recent occurrence in the drawing-room, which she had completely forgotten, neither did she mention the notice to ber daughter. The latter probably saw it herself, however, although she did not speak of it to Lady H. Both mother and daughter appeared anxious to avoid any allusion to the dead man of whom neither had any pleasant recollection.

About a week after the notice in the paper, Lady H. began to observe a change in her daughter's usual placid and cheerful manner. She had begun to grow nervous and wore an uneasy look. She made no complaints and at first eluded her mother's efforts to penetrate into what was wrong, but at last a mother's love and anxiety prevailed and Miss H. confessed that at intervals, in fact ever since the afternoon in the drawing-room, she had had an impression of the sound of approaching footsteps. These footsteps, she said, occurred at irregular intervals and at any time and place. They might be heard as she sat with her mother, or when she was out of doors or alone in her room. They always began some way off, approached hastily and, at first especially, rather irregularly and they always ceased at some little distance from her. What agitated her most was that the steps resembled those of the late Captain X. of whose memory she now felt a sickening fear and horror. Lady H., a practical, matter-of-fact woman, with no belief in what she called ghost humbug, was somewhat puzzled over her daughter's story, but on consideration put it down to fancy and a disturbed digestion, both of which she proceeded to treat, the former with advice and remonstrance, the latter with various simple remedies.

Miss H. grew no better under this treatment and Lady H. presently called in the services of their local doctor, a man of neither greater nor less ability than the mass of country practitioners. This gentleman also ascribed Miss H.'s trials to the purely physical causes of indigestion and followed in Lady H.'s footsteps in the matter of remedies with as little success as had attended her efforts. Miss H. grew worse and more nervous, and ultimately the local doctor, confessing his inability to deal properly with the case, recommended that the advice of a nerve specialist be asked and gave Lady H. the name and address of the well-known physician in London, who may now be left to tell the remainder of the story in his own words.

'On a certain date, which I need not more particularly specify, I received a letter from Dr B. of Atherfield, Hampshire, saying that he had requested Lady H. to bring her daughter to me for advice. Dr B.'s letter was not very clearly worded, but I gathered from it that Miss H. believed herself to be suffering from some form of haunting, a belief which Dr B. did not wholly share. His country medical experience had not afforded him opportunities of studying the numerous subtle varieties of psychic affections, or I might say afflictions, which torment sensitive and receptive minds. While, therefore, he attributed Miss H.'s trouble to physical causes primarily, which causes might affect the mental and nervous system, I was prepared from the first to consider that this was far more likely to be a case of mental disturbance reacting on the body.

'Well, in due course Lady H. wrote for an appointment for herself and her daughter, and presented herself and the young lady in my consulting room on the prescribed date. On a first inspection I was not seriously disturbed by Miss H.'s appearance. She looked in good health and her various organs were in good working order. I listened to her and her mother's stories and came to the conclusion that the probabilities pointed to the first sound of footsteps being genuinely clairaudient, that the late Captain X. had at the moment of his death, which I gathered was instantaneous, been deeply absorbed in the thought of Miss H., and that under laws which are known to exist, although by no means understood, had been transported spiritually to her neighbourhood and had become manifest by chair-audience to her during his approach. There are too many well-authenticated cases of apparitions at the point of death for us any longer to disbelieve in their possibility, but the continuance of such manifestations for any length of time after bodily extinction are, as has been shown by Mr Myers, of much more rare and less well-evidenced occurrence.

'Accordingly, whilst prepared to admit that in the first instance Miss H. had been the percipient of a genuine manifestation, I was inclined to believe that the subsequent recurrence of the footsteps was due to an unconscious agitation of her subconscious self and that they were genuine hallucinations, having no real existence. To remove those impressions it appeared to me desirable to prescribe a course of hypnotic suggestion; but I had no sooner hinted at this form of treatment than I found myself strongly opposed by Lady H., who emphatically declared her entire disbelief in and religious revolt from any such proceeding. Obliged to abandon the treatment, owing to this opposition, I fell back upon prescribing a tonic and a complete change of scene, and I advised Lady H. to take her daughter to the sea for a three weeks' stay and to let me know on her return how the patient did.

'The ladies promised to follow my directions and left me, after which I allowed the whole case to fade from my mind.

'Exactly three weeks later it was revived by the receipt of a letter from Lady H. written from her London house and asking me to call and see Miss H. as soon as possible, as they had returned from the sea with the trouble not only unabated but greatly increased.

'At the time I was very busy, but I managed to get round to — Street fairly early on the following morning. After a brief interview with Lady H., who was extremely agitated, I was shown up alone to Miss H.'s sitting-room, a pleasant apartment at the back of the house and approached by a short, oilcloth-covered passage.

'I was greatly shocked by the change in the young lady's appearance. Physically she had deteriorated greatly, as was apparent at the first glance, but mentally her condition was even more alarming. She had apparently lost all control over herself, trembled violently for no ostensible reason, and appeared to be constantly keenly listening for some dreaded sound. She greeted me eagerly and instantly began: "Oh, doctor, can you not help me? I know you thought when I saw you before you could do something, if only Mother would have allowed it; and now I will insist on doing anything you tell me, anything, if only I can be relieved from him."

' "Tell me more of your trouble," I said. "Are you still haunted by the sound of footsteps?"

' "Haunted," she said. "Haunted, yes, that is just the word. You know I told you I was troubled by footsteps coming from a distance and stopping well away from me. They did not come often then, but they do now; they come all the time," she went on, "and come clearer and louder and they come nearer. Nearer, nearer, they come close to me and, oh God, one day he will reach and touch me and then – "

She stopped for a moment and I was thinking what I could say to reassure her when she suddenly caught hold of my arm.

' "There they are now," she cried. "Listen, they are coming down the passage. Listen, listen."

'Her distress and agitation were so extreme that I could not control myself for a moment and we both sat in dead silence listening. I am not a nervous or imaginative man and in my cool moments I am sure I was mistaken; but at that instant I could have sworn that I heard a footfall on the oilcloth outside.

' "Do you hear him?" she cried again. "He is coming, oh, help me."

'I took her hands in mine and looked her steadily in the face. "Control yourself," I said. "You are safe, you cannot be harmed."

'As I spoke her look of [agitation vanished and] she said: "He has stopped; he has gone again – but he will come back. He will never really go away till he can take me too."

'I did my best to reassure her and presently she grew calmer and promised me that she would certainly not listen for the recurrence of the steps, and would endeavour to surround herself with a form of protective envelope, evolved out of her own inner thoughts and will power, so as to ward them off. I was, however, determined at once to commence a course of hypnotic suggestion; with the consent of Lady H. if possible, if not, without. Accordingly I went downstairs and after an earnest conversation with her at last I carried my point. I was then obliged to leave the house to attend to other pressing duties, but I settled to return that afternoon and commence the treatment. In the meantime I arranged with Lady H. that, pending my return, either she or some trusty servant should remain constantly with Miss H.

'That afternoon, in accordance with my promise, I returned to — Street to find the house in sad trouble, the butler, who opened the door, informing me that Miss H. had died suddenly a short time before. While talking to him about the event, I saw Dr K., a family physician of my acquaintance, descending the stairs. He greeted me and, telling me that he was the London medical attendant of the

H. family, took me into a room on the ground floor to tell me what details he could of the tragedy.

'It appeared that after my visit Miss H. had grown more cheerful and confident of herself. She had been quickly joined by her mother, and the two ladies had remained together till after luncheon, when they went into the drawing-room. A short time after this Lady H. was called to the telephone and, knowing that her absence would be short and thinking Miss H. might, in her happier frame of mind, be left for this brief space of time, she went downstairs to the instrument, leaving Miss H. lying on a sofa alone in the drawing-room. Lady H. had just finished her conversation and was hanging up the receiver when she was startled by hearing a loud scream for help. She rushed upstairs to find Miss H. stretched on the floor in a corner of the room some distance from her sofa, dead.

'After a few questions had been asked and answered, I asked Dr K. for his opinion as to the cause of death, and he replied: "Heart failure, undoubtedly caused in my opinion by a shock; but I can form no opinion as to its nature, as there was nothing in Miss H.'s surroundings in the drawing-room of an unusual or alarming character."

'He presently offered to allow me to inspect the body, and I can only say that I have never seen on any living or dead face such an agonised look of fear and horror as on that of the dead girl.'

The Young Lady in Black

The following story is one of actual experience, and while not a tale of horror and woe, like the typical ghost story, still is interesting as opening up for consideration the question whether, after the death of the body, the spirit is able to carry on and bring to a more or less satisfactory conclusion some task commenced in the flesh. While it is certainly very much open to doubt whether for indefinite ages the spirit revisits the scenes of its earthly career and repeats over and over again, frequently for no apparent reason, certain episodes in that career; yet, to those who believe that the body is a mere cloak or garment covering the real man within, it may appear highly credible that the spirit of a human being who has suddenly been cut off in the midst of some special earthly task may be able to revisit this earth, and complete his work.

In a story such as this, it is not opportune to discuss the relations between soul and body, but instances of second sight or the apparition of some person at the moment of his decease to some distant friend are so numerous, and are frequently so well authenticated that it is almost impossible not to believe them.

The following story was told to the present writer in sober earnestness by a man whose integrity is indubitable. That the narrator may have been mistaken is quite possible, but that he firmly believed what he narrated is without question, and if he really is correct in his story, and did not unconsciously add to its marvellous features, after he had learned the truth, it would seem that it is a piece of strong evidence that occasionally the dead, to accomplish some particular end, *are* permitted to revisit the earth and become visible to some at least of its living inhabitants. Here is the story.

One afternoon I was busily engaged in my studio in London, working at a picture I was very anxious to finish. I had not suffered myself to be disturbed all day and now was feeling rather tired, but very pleased at the rapid progress I was making.

Presently I heard a ring at the door-bell, and after the lapse of a few moments my servant entered. I was annoyed at being disturbed and asked the man rather sharply what he wanted.

'Sir,' he replied. 'There is a lady in the drawing-room who is very anxious to see you. I told her you were engaged, but she would take no excuse and said she must see you.'

'What is her name, and what does she want?' I asked. 'Tell her I am sorry, but I cannot be disturbed without good reason.'

He went away, and in a few minutes returned. 'The lady won't give her name, sir,' he said. 'As for her business, she says it's very important, and that you will be glad enough to see her.'

'Well, show her up.'

The servant again departed, and in a few moments ushered the lady into the studio. I looked at her and saw a woman somewhat over medium height, with small hands and feet, and of a ladylike demeanour. She was dressed entirely in black and wore a heavy black veil, which completely concealed her face. I judged from her general appearance, however, that she was a lady, and a total stranger. I motioned her to a seat and stood waiting for her to speak, which she at once began to do.

'You are very kind, Mr M., to give me a few moments, I see you are very busy, but I won't detain you long,' she said, in a soft, well-modulated voice. 'I am come to ask you to undertake the painting of a portrait.'

I bowed, but said nothing.

'Your reputation,' the lady continued 'is widespread, and that is one of the principal reasons why I have applied to you, for the portrait will be rather a difficult one to paint.'

I murmured something in acquiescence, and she went on: 'The person I want you to portray is myself. I am willing and able to agree to any pecuniary terms you may name, but I wish the portrait to be very carefully and expeditiously done.'

I named my terms, and added: 'Will you kindly allow me to see your face, madam, I shall then be able to judge better whether I can undertake the task.'

'Certainly,' she replied, and threw back her veil disclosing a very striking face. It was that of a woman of apparently about thirty years of age of a noble bearing, tempered, however, with an appearance of constant suffering. In the deep, dark eyes there was a fixed expression of trouble, hopeless and endless; on the lofty brow there were the tokens of pride hardly yet subdued by grief. Round the mouth played a strange smile, indescribable almost, an expression of deep sorrow and unavailing regret. She looked like one who had passed through the valley of the shadow of death and knew the full mysteries of that awful vale.

For an instant I shrank back with a sort of shudder, not that the face was repulsive, but that there was in it an unearthly something impossible to describe. However, ardour for my art soon got the better of my former feeling, and I answered: 'Madam, I shall be very glad to undertake your portrait, though you have so unusual an expression that it will be a hard one to paint. Still I will do my best. When and where do you want to sit?'

She smiled slightly, and said: 'Mr M., perhaps you will decline at once, when I must try elsewhere, but I will tell you now frankly that I am not able to give you any sittings at all.'

'What?' I cried. 'Why, I cannot paint you without your sitting to me.'

'Well,' she answered, 'that cannot be done. All I can do is to sit here now for half an hour or so and let you look at me and sketch me, and then leave this little portrait of myself with you.'

She took from her pocket a little watercolour of herself, which had apparently been torn from some book. It had been taken when she was about eighteen, and before the strange expression had come into her face; it was, however, very like her, only the colouring was fresh and rosy.

'Well,' I said as I took it, 'I will see what I can do in so short a time, though I am afraid I shall make a poor job of it.'

So saying, I sat down and sketched her as carefully and as rapidly as possible though I found great difficulty in catching the various expressions of her face.

In about half an hour she rose, saying: 'I must go now, Mr M., many thanks for your kindness, here is the price you named for the picture. You see I can trust you, and will pay in advance.' With these words she counted out a sum of money in banknotes on the table, and gave me an address to which she wished the picture to be sent. 'Now,' she added, 'I know I have asked you to undertake a very difficult piece of work, but I am not mistress of my own movements. If at any time I find myself able to give you another sitting I will certainly do so; if not,' she went on pleadingly, 'I beg you will do your best to try and make a likeness of me; it is important, most important. Goodbye.'

And before I could move or speak she was out of the room. I rang for the servant to show her out, but on his arrival he said he had not seen the lady, and supposed that she must have left the house in a hurry. I put the two sketches away intending to commence work on them as soon as I had leisure, but, an important commission coming in next day, they slipped my memory entirely for some little time.

About three months after the above events, I found a note awaiting me on the breakfast table one morning from my old friend Arthur Van C. inviting me to come and visit him and his wife at their house about twenty miles from Ipswich. As I had no pressing work to do at that time, and felt that I needed a rest, I decided to accept their invitation, more especially as the Van C.'s had only recently returned from a five years' sojourn in India, and I was anxious to see him again.

Two or three hours saw me complete my arrangements in London, and found me landed at the Liverpool Street terminus, seeking in that vast labyrinth the express for Ipswich. I found my train at length, and ensconced myself in an empty first-class carriage which, with the aid of a couple of shillings, I proposed to keep to myself all the way down. But I was doomed to disappointment. Just before the train started, the door of my carriage was opened, a porter's voice said 'Here, y'are, ma'am,' and a tall lady dressed in deep mourning entered the compartment. There was something about her which appeared familiar to me, but I did not recognise her till, soon after the train had left the station, she raised her veil, and disclosed my fair visitor of three months before. I was at first startled, and then a feeling of shame rushed over me. I had taken this lady's money and promised to paint her picture at once, and here at the expiration of three months not a brush had been laid to canvas. I did not know what to say, but finally bowed and murmured a greeting. She responded, and promptly asked: 'Well, Mr M., when will you finish my picture?'

This completely disconcerted me; I inwardly vowed I would work incessantly on that portrait till it was finished, while aloud I said: 'My dear madam, I have been so busy that really I have had but little time.'

'I feared as much,' she interrupted me, 'but I do beg, Mr M., that you will take the matter up in earnest when you return to town. You don't know, you can't guess, what a weight will be off my mind when that picture is finished.'

'I promise you,' I replied, 'that I will have it done very quickly. I will give it precedence over all other work.'

'I hope you will,' she said, and then added, 'I am glad to have this opportunity afforded me to let you look at my face and gather some ideas for the picture.'

I replied that I also was pleased to have the chance, and added: 'And also to have the pleasure of travelling down with you into Suffolk.' She smiled, and we had a pleasant conversation during our journey to Ipswich, though I found that my companion's part in it was at all times tinged with a certain sadness. At Ipswich station I lost sight of her in the confusion incidental on changing trains, and it was not till I was seated in the little branch railway that I bethought myself that I had forgotten to ask her name or ascertain her destination.

However, I dismissed the subject, and on my arrival at Pocklington, the station nearest Van C.'s house, I found myself so busy hunting up luggage and a conveyance that I completely forgot my fellow traveller. After a drive of some three miles, I arrived about half-past seven at Van C.'s house, and on the door being opened was greeted by the butler, who said: 'Dinner will soon be ready, Mr M. The family is upstairs dressing. I will show you to your room at once, sir, if you please.'

I went up, therefore, immediately, and with the assistance of the butler rapidly unpacked and dressed for dinner. I mention these comparatively trivial circumstances to show what good ground for surprise I had at what next befell me. Upon descending to the library, where I expected to find my host and hostess, I saw, standing with her back towards me, a tall lady dressed in a black evening gown. On hearing me enter she turned round, and for an instant I was struck dumb with amazement, for she was none other than my late travelling companion. I had never seen Mrs Van C. and I at once concluded that this must be she, but how in the name of wonder had she got here, and why had she not introduced herself to me in the train?

'Well, this is an unexpected pleasure, Mrs Van C.,' I exclaimed. 'I never dreamed it was my future hostess I was talking to this afternoon.'

'I am not Mrs Van C.,' she answered.

But before she had time to say more the door opened, and Van C., accompanied by a lady, came in. He shook hands with me heartily, and introduced the lady with him as his wife, but I was a little surprised to notice that neither of them spoke to my companion. However, I at once concluded that she was some governess or lady companion of Mrs Van C. and seeing that they ignored her presence I decided it might be proper for me to do so also. At this moment dinner was announced, and Van C. asked his wife if she expected Mr Brixham, to which she replied that she had had a place set for him but did not know if he would come.

'At any rate,' she concluded, 'we won't wait. Will you take me in, Mr M?' And as we went in to dinner she explained to me that Mr Brixham was the clergyman of the parish, and had a standing invitation to dine with them.

We entered the dining-room, and I saw the table was set for four persons. I led Mrs Van C. to the head of the table, and while seating herself she dropped her handkerchief; I stooped to pick it up, and by the time I regained my seat saw Van C. and the lady of the train in their respective places, Van. C. opposite his wife, and the mysterious lady opposite to myself. In the centre of the table was a large vase supporting a basket of flowers, and decked with hanging garlands, which effectually shut off my view of all but the top of the head of my opposite neighbour. Dinner commenced, and I found Van C., as he had always been, one of the most jovial and talkative of men, whilst his wife, also, was by no means lacking in conversational powers. Van C. kept me pretty busy all through dinner talking about old times, and though I could not help noticing that neither he nor his wife ever spoke to the strange lady, yet I did not have an opportunity of addressing myself directly to her. I am not much of an observer and, as I say, my attention was pretty constantly taken up, yet it was my impression that my opposite neighbour partook of the good things set before her, and I became at last firmly impressed with the idea that she must be Mrs Van C.'s companion.

At the end of dinner Van C. opened the door to the retiring ladies, and as soon as he had resumed his seat I determined to satisfy my curiosity as to my fair client, and said: 'By the way, Van C., I wish you would introduce me to that lady who has just gone out. I travelled part of the way from London with her today, and have engaged myself to paint her portrait also.'

I shall never be able to paint such surprise as overspread Van C.'s face. 'What?' he said. 'You travelled from London today with my wife, and are going to paint her picture?'

'No, no,' I said, 'not your wife, I mean the other lady, the one who sat opposite to me.'

'The one who sat opposite to you?' Van C. repeated. 'Why, my dear fellow, the seat opposite to you was empty.'

'Empty?' I cried. 'Are you blind, Van C., or are you joking? I tell you I mean the seat on the opposite side of the table to myself that was occupied by that striking-looking woman in black.'

'You are mad,' retorted Van C. 'No one sat opposite to you. There was a seat there for Mr Brixham, but he didn't come, and there was no one in the room all through dinner except ourselves, my wife, and the servants.'

'But I saw her,' I persisted.

'You can't have seen her,' he said, 'because she wasn't there. Come into the drawing-room and we'll ask my wife, if you don't believe me.'

'Well,' I said, 'here is some extraordinary mistake. Let's go and ask Mrs Van C. to decide it.' So to the drawing-room we adjourned, and on entering it I saw that Mrs Van C. was alone.

'Now, Emily,' cried her husband, 'M. and I have had a dispute and we are going to leave it to you to decide. Was there or was there not a handsome lady dressed in black sitting opposite M. at dinner tonight?'

'No,' answered Mrs Van C. in surprise, 'there was nothing but Mr Brixham's vacant place.'

'There, I told you so,' cried Van C. 'Now if you like we'll have the servants up and ask them.'

'I wish you would, Van. C.,' I answered, 'there's some strange mystery here which I should like to have cleared up.'

So the servants were summoned, and Van C. told me to ask what questions I liked.

'Was there,' I began, 'any lady at table tonight besides Mrs Van C.?'

The butler and footman stared at me in great astonishment, and then said, 'No, sir.'

'And there was no one at all opposite to me?' I continued.

And the answer again came, 'No, sir.'

'There was a place set?' I queried.

'Yes, sir, for Mr Brixham, but he didn't come, so we took it down,' replied the butler.

I thanked the men and let them go. I asked Mr and Mrs Van C. if a person such as I described had lived in the house at any time, but though I gave a lengthy and I am sure an accurate description, they utterly failed to recognise her. Finding therefore that I had evidently been the subject of some strange hallucination, I determined to endeavour to think no more of it. I decided to paint the picture of the mysterious lady at once and send it to the address in Ipswich she had given me, accompanying it by a note begging her to favour me with some explanation as to how and why she had caused, if she indeed knew the reason, an image of herself to appear to me.

The chief point of difficulty I met with, in my endeavours to solve the mystery, was the impossibility of deciding *when* the hallucination commenced. Was the whole affair a hallucination, or did the deception begin in the railway train or not until I arrived at Van C.'s house? And another point was, why had the deception been practised at all? Finally I came to the conclusion that I had really travelled with the lady from London, principally because I heard and saw the porter usher her into the train in London, and that during the journey her figure and face had impressed itself so strongly upon me, as indeed she must have wished it to do, that I had imagined the scene at dinner. Curiously enough, I was not during the whole of this time in the least degree alarmed, but only looked forward to another meeting with my friend, intending to wring some sort of explanation from her.

Full of this determination I fell asleep, and passed a perfectly uneventful night. In the morning the Van C.'s rallied me a good deal about my friend of the night before, and when I explained to them my theories listened to me with evident incredulity.

My visit to the Van C.'s passed off very pleasantly, and I was heartily sorry to return to London. I was not again visited by my strange acquaintance's *eidolon*, and in fact began to believe she had lost her power to appear to me.

On the day of my return to London, I somehow missed the connecting train at Ipswich, and found myself with several hours to spare in that not particularly interesting town. But determined to make the best use I could of my time, I took my portfolio of sketches, and with a few pencils strolled forth from the station in quest of some object of interest. These, however, were rare, and I quickly found myself in great danger of boredom when I suddenly remembered that an old friend, whom I had lost sight of for many, many years, lived in Ipswich, and I at once determined to look him up. I enquired for Mr J.'s house, to which I was directed, and soon found myself knocking at the door. It was opened by a young and rather pretty girl, whose face I somehow seemed to know though I had never seen her to my knowledge. I enquired for Mr J. and mentioned my name.

'Come in,' she said. 'I will go and see my father and find out if he will see you. He has been very strange ever since my sister's death about four months ago, and doesn't like visitors.'

I was pleased with her sweet face and, besides having nothing to do, really wanted to see her father, so I entered and sat down in a pretty little parlour while she went upstairs. In a few minutes she reappeared, saying: 'Father is coming down. He wouldn't do so at first, but when he heard who you were said he would. I think,' she added, 'he is going to ask you for something, so please don't be angry.'

'Angry?' I said. 'Why should I be angry?'

'Well,' she answered, 'Father has been very queer since my sister Rose died, and always wanting to have something to remind him of her, a picture most particularly. He once said he was going to write and ask you to paint one, but, oh dear, the little sketch that we used to have has been lost, and that,' she added plaintively, 'was the only likeness we had of her.'

As she finished speaking her father – my old friend J. – entered the room. He shook me warmly by the hand, but I noticed at once in his manner something strange and unsettled. He sat down, and for a minute or two we spoke of indifferent subjects, but all at once he broke out: 'Oh, M., my good friend, you can help me, and you only. Cannot you paint her, just a little picture, only a little one.'

'I would like to, J.,' I answered, 'but it is pretty difficult unless you have some photograph to give me. Your daughter here has been telling me that you want a picture of your eldest child, but says you have lost the only sketch you had.'

'Yes, yes,' murmured J. 'And I shall never see her again.'

I pitied his distress, and more to soothe him than anything said: 'Cannot you describe your daughter, J.? Perhaps I could do something from your description.'

'Yes,' he cried eagerly, 'perhaps you could. Oh, she was so pretty, so sweet: dark brown eyes, and such black hair, never had anyone hair like Rose.'

I cannot tell what prompted me, some strange, unseen influence it certainly must have been, for taking my portfolio I unbuckled it, and producing the sketch given me by my strange visitor the first time she came to my studio I handed it to J. saying: 'Did she resemble this sketch, J.?'

For a few moments J. and his daughter gazed at the sketch with the blankest amazement; at last J. managed to articulate: 'Where did you get this?'

'A lady gave it to me about three or four months ago,' I answered, 'she came to my studio to ask me to paint her, and as she was unable to give me any sittings left me this sketch to work from. I saw her again a few days ago, and she begged me to hasten on with my work. Here are one or two sketches I have taken of her.'

'This is my daughter's portrait,' cried J. as he glanced at the sketches. 'In God's name when did you see her?'

'I saw her first in my studio just about fourteen weeks ago,' I replied, 'when she gave me an order to paint her picture and send it to – Great Heaven! why, it was this address, 14 Colchester Street, she gave me at the time she handed me this little sketch of herself.'

'When did you miss the picture, Alice?' cried her father.

'Just fourteen weeks ago today,' answered Miss J. 'I was looking through the portfolio and found it was not there.'

'Great are God's ways,' said J. after a few moments' silence. 'My daughter Rose died just four months ago; she had long been failing, and it was my special wish that she should have her picture taken. She kept on delaying it till it was too late.'

My story is now ended, and I will close it as I commenced it, by asking whether there is any returning for a specified purpose? Perhaps there may be, perhaps, as in the quaint, weird story of old Lady Mary there may be a returning, a returning of the loved one to wander in silence and unperceived amongst us, bearing as his punishment for some unexpiated fault the bitter grief of seeing those he has loved suffering under unmerited wrong. Perhaps even as this is written and this is read the spirits of the departed are hovering silent and unseen near the writer and the reader, perhaps guiding the hand to write, and the eye to read, perhaps, unhappy that they be, only conscious of the griefs to fall on the mortals before them and unable to avert the impending calamities. These things can never be known. Suffice it now to say that the narrator of the above story believed it to be true, and that he actually painted the portrait of the dead Rose J., partly from the little sketch and partly from the remembrance of her face as he saw it. Herself he never saw more: the mission for which she had been permitted to revisit the earth was accomplished, the fault she had committed in neglecting her father's wishes had doubtless been expiated, and her troubled soul rested in peace.

Two last pieces of evidence as to the truth of this strange story may be adduced in the testimony of the porter at Liverpool Street railway station, who distinctly remembered that the part of the platform where he had been standing was empty, and that suddenly he heard a lady's voice say: 'Porter, in this carriage please,' and turning, had seen a lady in black pointing to M.'s carriage.

The servant also at Mr M.'s remembered admitting her to the studio.

The Downs

I am venturing to set down the following personal experience, inconclusive as it is, as I feel that it may interest those who have the patience to study the phenomena of the unseen world around us. It was my first experience of a psychical happening and its events are accordingly indelibly imprinted on my memory.

The date was, alas, a good many years ago, when I was still a young man and at the time was engaged in reading hard for a certain examination. My friend J. was in similar plight to myself and together we decided to abjure home and London life and seek a quiet country spot, where we might devote ourselves to our work amidst pleasant and congenial surroundings.

J. knew of such a place: a farm belonging to a Mr Harkness, who was a distant connection of his own by marriage. Mr Harkness was a childless widower and lived much to himself at Branksome Farm, attended to only by an elderly housekeeper and one or two servants. Although he called himself a farmer and did in fact farm fairly extensively, he was a man of cultivated and even learned tastes, widely read and deeply versed in the history and folklore of his neighbourhood. At the same time, although good-natured, he was the most reserved and tactiturn man I ever met, and appeared to have a positive horror of communicating his very considerable fund of local knowledge to outsiders like ourselves. However, he was glad to welcome us as paying guests for the sake of his relationship to J., and he and his housekeeper certainly took great care to make us comfortable and happy.

Branksome Farm is a large old-fashioned house, surrounded by the usual farm buildings and situated in a valley winding its way among the Downs. The situation is beautiful and remote, and it would astonish many of our City dwellers to know that within two or three hours' railway journey from London there still are vast stretches of open downland on which one may walk for hours without sight of a human being, and traversed only by winding roads which run from one small town or hamlet to another, linking a few lonely cottages or farms to civilisation on their route. Behind the house Branksome Down, the highest in the neighbourhood, rises steeply, and beyond it at a distance of about three miles is Willingbury, the nearest town, whence the railway runs to London.

It is necessary to describe the geography of the country between Willingbury and Branksome a little more closely. The two places lie, as is usually the case in the Down country, in valleys between the hills and by road are distant from each other about six to seven miles, being separated by the long ridge of Branksome Down. But actually the distance between them does not exceed three miles across the Down: the path from Branksome, a mere sheep-track, leading up to the top of Branksome Down whence the wanderer sees before him a wide shallow dip in the Down, nearly circular, about three-quarters of a mile across and at the other side sloping up to another gentle ridge. Arrived at the summit of this second elevation the traveller gazes down on the Willingbury-Overbury road and following another sheep-track down the hillside he reaches the road about a mile outside Willingbury.

The whole Down is covered with sweet, short turf, unbroken by trees or shrubs and, at the time of my story, was unmarred by fencing of any form. Flocks of sheep tended by shepherds and their watchful dogs were almost its sole inhabitants, save for the shy, wild life that clings to all natural shelters. Of the beauty of this Down and, in fact, of the whole neighbourhood it is useless to speak. To anyone who has once felt the fascination of a walk in the fresh, pure air, over the springy and centuries-old turf, and who has allowed his eyes to wander over the miles and miles of open Down, studded here and there with rare belts of trees, and has watched the shifting lights play over the near and distant hills, it is needless to speak, and to anyone who has never yet been fortunate enough to find himself in downland in fine weather one can hardly make its fascination clear in words, and one can only advise him to go and explore its beauties for himself.

Well, it was at Branksome Farm that J. and I took up our abode and commenced a course of steady reading, tempered and varied by long walks about the country. Our time passed pleasantly and profitably, and we discovered one day with regret that more than half of it had elapsed. Dismayed at this discovery we began to set our wits to work to find an excuse for prolonging our stay at Branksome, when suddenly an event happened which entirely altered our plans.

Returning one day from our accustomed walk, J. found a telegram waiting for him, which called him to London without delay and the contents of which appeared to indicate the probability of his being unable to return to Branksome. No time was to be lost in making a start if he was to catch the afternoon train at Willingbury and, as it was really quicker to walk across the Down than to drive round the roads behind Mr Harkness' rather slow old mare, he threw a few clothes hastily into a bag and departed for the station. I accompanied him to see him off and we made the best possible speed to Willingbury. But we had miscalculated the time; the afternoon train had gone, and we found on enquiry that there would be no other until the night mail for London, which passed through Willingbury shortly before 11 p.m.

J. urged me not to wait for this but to leave him at the little inn and go back to Branksome before dark, but I was anxious to keep him company and cheer up his rather depressed spirits, so finally we agreed to dine together at the *Blue Lion* and spend the evening there until the train left. I was perfectly confident in my ability to find my way back over the Down to Branksome at night, as the path was very familiar to us, and I expected to be aided by the light of the moon which would rise about ten o'clock. In due course the train arrived, and having seen J. safely on his way to London I turned my steps towards the Willingbury-Overbury road and its junction with the Branksome sheeptrack.

It was a little after 11 p.m. when I left Willingbury on my homeward way, and I was disappointed to find that the moon had failed me, being completely hidden behind a thick canopy of cloud. The night was profoundly still as well as being very dark, but I was confident in my powers of finding my way and I strode contentedly along the road till I reached the point where it was necessary I should diverge on to the Down. I found the commencement of the sheeptrack without difficulty, as my eyes were now accustomed to the surrounding obscurity, and set myself to climbing the Down as quickly as possible.

I must make it clear that up to the present time I had been in my usual state of health and spirits, although the latter were somewhat depressed at J.'s sudden departure and the break-up of our pleasant association together. Up to this night, also, I had never in the least suspected that I was possessed of any special psychic intelligence. It is true that I had known that I was in the habit of occasionally dreaming very vividly and consecutively, but I had never given this faculty a serious thought, nor, like most young men in their twenties, had I ever given any consideration to psychic matters. It must be remembered also that I am writing of nearly forty years ago, when an intelligent interest in the potentialities of unseen beings and kindred topics was far less common than it is today.

Well, I commenced my ascent of the hill, and I had not gone very far when I became aware of a certain peculiar change taking place in myself. I fear I shall find it very difficult to describe my sensations in a fashion intelligible to those who have never experienced anything similar, whilst to those who have undergone psychic ordeals my description will probably appear bald and inadequate.

I seemed to be in some mysterious fashion divided into a dual personality. One, the familiar one, was myself, my body, which continued to walk up the sheep-track, keenly alive to the need to keep a sharp look out against losing my way or stumbling over some obstruction. This personality also felt loneliness and a certain degree of nervousness. The darkness, silence and immensity of the empty country round me were oppressive. I feared something, I was not quite sure what, and I anxiously wished I was at the end of my journey with the farm lights shining out to welcome me. My other personality was more vague and ill-defined; it seemed to be separated from my body and from my outer consciousness and to be floating in a region where there was neither space nor time. It seemed to be aware of another world, a world surrounding and intermingling with this one, in which all that is or was or will be was but one moment and in which all places near or far, the Down and the remotest of the invisible stars, were but one spot. All was instantaneous and all was eternal. I am not clear how long this mood lasted, but it was probably only a few minutes before my earthly self was brought or appeared to be brought into entire control of my personality by a sudden shock.

As I walked I became aware that I was not alone. There was a man moving parallel with me on my right at the distance of some four or five yards. So suddenly and so silently had he appeared that he seemed to have risen from the earth. He was walking quite quietly at my own pace abreast of me, but apparently taking no notice of me, and I observed that his footsteps made no sound on the soft turf. The dim light made it difficult to see him at all distinctly, but he was evidently a tall, powerfully built fellow, dressed in a long cloak, which, partly covering his face, fell nearly to his feet. On his head he wore a queer-shaped, three-cornered hat and in his hand he carried what appeared to be a short, heavy bludgeon.

I was greatly startled. I am a small and by no means robust man and the apparition of this odd-looking stranger on these lonely Downs was disquieting. What did he want? Had he followed me down the road from Willingbury, and, if so, for what purpose? However, I decided it was best not to appear alarmed and after taking another glance at the man, I wished him good evening.

He took not the faintest notice of my salutation, which he appeared not even to have heard, but continued to advance up the hill by my side in dead silence.

After a few moments I spoke again; and this time my voice sounded strange in my own ears, as if it did not come from my lips, but from somewhere far away. 'A dark night,' I said.

And now he answered. In a slow, measured voice, but one in which there sounded a note of hopelessness and misery, he said: 'It is dark to you. It is darker for me.'

I scarcely knew what to reply, but I felt that my courage was at an ebb and that I must maintain it by endeavouring to keep up a conversation, difficult though this might prove. Accordingly I went on: 'This is a strange place to walk in at night. Have you far to go?'

He did not turn his head or look at me. 'Your way is short and easy, but mine is long and hard. How long, O Lord, how long?' he cried.

As he uttered the last words his voice rose to a cry and he tossed his arms above his head, letting them fall to his side with a gesture of despair.

We had now almost reached the top of the Down, and as we neared the summit I became aware that the wind was rising. At the moment we were sheltered from it by the brow of the hill, but I could hear its distant roaring, and as we reached the summit it broke upon us with a rush.

With it and mingled in its sounds came other sounds, the sounds of human voices, of many voices, in many keys. There were sounds of wailing, of shouting, of chanting, of sobbing, even at times of laughter. The great, shallow bowl of Branksome Down was alive with sounds. I could see nothing, save my strange companion, who continued to move steadily forward; and I, dreading his company and yet dreading even more to be left alone, accompanied him. The night was still profoundly dark, and though as I advanced the voices often sounded quite near, I saw nothing until after we had passed the centre of the depression and were mounting the opposite slope. At that moment the wind tore aside the clouds and the moon streamed down full upon the Downs. By her light I saw a marvellous and a terrifying sight. The whole of Branksome Down was alive with people hurrying hither and thither, some busy and absorbed in their occupations, whatever they might be, others roaming aimlessly and tossing their arms into the air with wild and tragic gesticulations. The crowd appeared to be of all sorts and conditions and to be dressed in the fashions of all the ages, though ancient costumes seemed to predominate. Here I saw a group of persons clothed apparently in the priestly robes of ancient Britain; there walked a soldier wearing the eagle-crested helmet of Rome. Other groups there were in dresses of later date, the steel-clad knight of the Middle Ages, the picturesque dress and flowing hair of a cavalier of the Seventeenth Century. But it was impossible to fix the shifting crowd. As I gazed, absorbed, at one figure, it melted and was gone and another took its place, to fade likewise as I watched.

My companion paid no heed to the throng. Steadily he passed on towards the crest of the hill, at intervals raising his arms and letting them fall with his old gesture of despair and uttering at the same time his mournful cry of 'How long, how long?'

We passed onward and upward and reached the top of the Down, my companion now a few yards in front of me. As he reached the crest of the hill, he stopped and, lifting his arms above his head, stood motionless. Suddenly he wavered, his figure expanded, its lines became vague and blurred against the background, it faded and was gone. As it vanished the wind dropped suddenly, the sound of human voices ceased and gazing round me I saw the plain bare and still in the moonlight.

I was now at the top of the hill, and looking downwards I saw a light burning in a window of Branksome Farm. I stumbled down the hill in haste, and as I approached the house saw Mr Harkness standing at the open door. He looked at me strangely as I entered.

'Have you come across Branksome Down tonight,' he exclaimed, 'tonight of all the nights in the year?'

'Yes,' I replied.

'I should have warned you,' he said, 'but I expected you back before dark. Branksome Down is an ill place tonight and men have vanished upon it before now and never been heard of again. No shepherd will set foot upon it tonight, for this is the night in the year when, folk say, all those that ever died violent deaths upon the Downs come back to seek their lost rest.'

The Late Mrs Fowke

The Reverend Barnabas Fowke, though he live to reach a century, will never forget the deathbed of his wife. Most widowers can probably say the same thing; though few, it may be hoped, have similar cause to recollect it.

Mr Fowke, at the time of the event referred to, was a man of middle age, and the incumbent of G., a small agricultural town on the edge of one of our Northern moors. He was a hard-working, honest parson, of no great strength of character and of no particular ability, nor had he had any special experience with the more subtle side of life. He had been educated at a good second-class public school and a small Oxford College, whence he had gone in due course to take up a curacy in one of our lesser manufacturing towns.

After serving some years in this capacity, he had been promoted, on the death of the vicar, to take charge of the living, in which position he had remained till a few weeks before his marriage to Stella Farnleigh, at whose instigation he had exchanged his town living at R. for the country one at G. which he still occupied at the time of this story. The reverend gentleman's history is thus commonplace and uninteresting, as, I fear, are the histories of many of our clergy, which it resembled save that, unlike most of his cloth, he had remained unmarried till he fell a victim at the age of forty to the charms of Miss Stella Farnleigh.

This lady requires a closer study. She was the only child of a certain Mr Farnleigh, who for many years was a merchant of, and acted as British Consul in, Z., a town in Hungary, where by hard work and close attention to business he amassed a fair-sized fortune. Somewhat late in life he had met a beautiful and attractive woman, whose nationality even was uncertain, but who boasted of a considerable admixture of gipsy blood in her veins. Exactly who she was or where she came from is at this distance of time impossible to ascertain. At the time she met Mr Farnleigh she was giving music lessons, by which she gained a small pittance, and her marriage to the well-to-do English merchant may well be considered a very fortunate event for her.

However, her married life did not last long, for Mr Farnleigh died very suddenly within six months of the wedding day, leaving his widow his sole executrix and legatee. It is not known whether Mrs Farnleigh had any relatives; if she had she never kept up any connection with them, and after her husband's death she acquired a small and lonely estate on the banks of the River Theiss and removed thither to dwell in complete retirement. Here in due course Stella was born and here the child lived with her mother until about the age of twenty-five, when Mrs Farnleigh died, leaving her fortune entirely to the girl.

The latter at first appeared to be inclined to remain on in her old home, but it would seem as if neither she nor her mother had been popular in the district, and apparently some pretty strong hints were conveyed to the young lady that she had best betake herself elsewhere. Mr Fowke knew nothing of all this at the time he married Stella, and for reasons which will transpire he did not care to make any investigations into the matter later on. Therefore the history of mother and daughter in Hungary and the reasons why the latter left that country are buried in an obscurity which will never be lightened. Whatever they may have been, Stella no doubt felt that it would be difficult for her to settle down by herself in any new country, and she accordingly put herself into communication with the only relative she knew herself possessed of, a Miss Farnleigh, the elderly sister of her father, with a view to taking up her abode with her as a paying guest.

The elder Miss Farnleigh was a poor woman, living in solitude at R. She was a worthy soul, narrow-minded, unintelligent, devoted to clergymen and church work; in fact, an absolute type of thousands of middle-aged, middle-class English spinsters. The proposal of her niece, whom she had never seen and with whom she had but rarely corresponded, was a welcome one, as the young lady would certainly provide some much-needed cash for the household, and would probably, as she fondly believed, provide a pleasant companion for herself also. Besides, she was sorry for the orphaned girl, and altogether it was with pleasure she made the preliminary arrangements and welcomed the arrival of the traveller.

However, these high hopes were doomed to disappointment. Stella and her aunt quickly found that they were uncongenial in nearly every respect. Miss Farnleigh I have described, and when I say that Stella was a young woman of considerable though rather peculiar literary accomplishments, and that she had a strong will which she frequently exercised in the pursuit of some highly unconventional purpose, I think it will be clear why the two ladies did not agree together. Stella had brought with her from Hungary a considerable library of foreign books, none of which her aunt could understand, but which actually dealt largely with occult subjects, and she also brought with her a habit of going away alone every few weeks for a night on the moors not far from R., a custom which she said she found necessary for her health and happiness. To these occasional expeditions Miss Farnleigh at first took great exception, but after a stormy scene with her niece the elder lady felt herself worsted and, as she had ceased to take any affectionate interest in the younger woman, she also ceased to care greatly as to what she did or thought. Stella, therefore, went on her own way undisturbed but conscious of perpetual criticism, and no doubt was eager to escape from an atmosphere so uncongenial to her. At the same time she realised the conventions that bound her and that her best hope for the future lay in marrying some man, weaker than herself, whom she could bend to her will. This, no doubt, actuated her in encouraging the somewhat timid suit of Mr Fowke, and in astonishing as well as delighting that gentleman when she accepted his rather diffident offer of marriage.

The young lady showed herself of an obliging disposition in the arrangements made prior to the wedding, her only stipulation being that Mr Fowke should change his present living for one nearer the moors. In accordance with this Mr Fowke negotiated an exchange with the vicar of G., and after a short honeymoon took possession of his new cure. Here he settled down to what he anticipated would prove a peaceful and happy life. He was devoted to his new wife, and she, while less demonstratively happy, appeared to be contented both with her husband and her new surroundings.

The first flaw in their married life showed itself a few months after their arrival at G., when one day, Mr Fowke, having occasion to speak to his wife, went upstairs to the room which she had selected as her private sitting-room and in which she had installed her voluminous library. On reaching it he heard from within a sound of low chanting in a language that he did not understand, and at the same time became aware of a singular smell as of the burning of some aromatic herb. He tried the door and, finding it locked, called to his wife. The chanting ceased immediately and his wife's voice told him to wait a few minutes and she would admit him. On the door being opened he found the room filled with a pungent smell emanating from some herbs, which were burning in a small brazier set upon the table.

'Whatever are you doing, my dear?' he asked.

Stella replied that she was suffering from a severe headache, which she was trying to cure by inhaling the smoke; it was an Hungarian remedy, she added, but she did not explain the singing. Mr Fowke remained somewhat puzzled, and his astonishment was considerably increased when a little later his wife informed him that she intended to go to L. – a tiny hamlet far up on the Fells – that afternoon and would spend the night there, returning the following day. It was the first time that Mr Fowke had heard of Stella's solitary visits to the moorland and he not unnaturally sought an explanation of them, which his wife refused to give in any greater detail than the mere statement that she had for long been accustomed to make these periodical trips into solitude. He asked to be allowed to accompany her, but she positively refused to permit this, and it was with a heavy and worried heart that he watched her leave the house later in the day.

The following afternoon she returned, tired and with muddy clothes, but seeming exhilarated by her expedition. She refused all information about it, save that during these trips she was in the habit of staying at the Three Magpies, a small inn at I., and making thence expeditions on the higher Fells. With this slender explanation Mr Fowke had to be satisfied.

A few weeks passed, when again one day Mr Fowke detected the odour of burning herbs and again learnt that his wife was on the point of starting for I. She again declined his proffered company and left the house as before.

Mr Fowke had never been to I., which is a remote hamlet, not distant as far as mileage is concerned from G., but only approachable by a branch line of railway with an infrequent service of trains. He was, however, acquainted with its vicar, to whom he presently wrote to enquire as to the standing of the Three Magpies, since he was not over-pleased that his wife, a foreigner ignorant of our ways, should elect to stay alone at an absolutely unknown inn. The reply he received was not at all reassuring, for the vicar of I. wrote that the

Three Magpies was a public house of poor repute, kept by an old couple of more than doubtful respectability.

This letter decided Mr Fowke and, when for the third time his wife announced her intention of proceeding to I. and for the third time refused his company, he determined to follow her there secretly and observe her movements and surroundings. It was not difficult for him to arrange to do this, since he could easily reach I. on his motor-cycle long before her slow train could land her there, even if he did not start until after she had left the parsonage. He carried out his programme and in due course reached I. and made his way to the Three Magpies. Here he found that the old man was very nearly bedridden and quite senile, whilst his wife regarded her clerical visitor with almost open hostility. However, the gift of a sovereign and the promise of another effected a great change and unlocked the old woman's tongue, so that she poured forth volubly all she knew.

Yes, she knew the lady quite well. She had been in the habit of coming to I. once every few weeks for a long time. No; she always came alone and had never spoken to anyone except herself, to her knowledge.

'What does she do?'

'Oh, she always goes straight up to her room and shuts herself in, then she sings to herself something I cannot make out and burns something that smells sweet and strong. About dark like, sometimes sooner, sometimes later, she comes down and goes out towards the Fells.'

'Have you ever followed her?'

'No, never, nor anybody else as I know of. A shepherd once saw her walking all alone in a wild part of the moor but he did not follow her or speak to her.'

'How long is she out?'

'Well, that depends, but generally till near morning. She takes the key of the house with her and lets herself in, but I hear her come in once in a while.'

'What does she do then?'

'Why, goes up to her room and stays there quietly and has break-fast and then goes to the train.'

This was about all that Mr Fowke could find out, except the curious detail that his wife never wore a hat on her nocturnal rambles, but went draped in a hooded grey cloak.

By the time this catechism was finished it was nearly time for Mrs Fowke to arrive, and the Reverend Barnabas accordingly ensconced himself in a room into which he was ushered by the old woman, which commanded the front door of the inn. In a short time he saw his wife arrive. After exchanging a few words with the old woman she went upstairs, and husband and wife remained in their respective seclusions till dusk fell.

Then Mr Fowke heard Stella descending the stairs and in a few moments he saw her emerge from the house clad, as described, in a long hooded grey cloak, and walking swiftly and resolutely. Giving her a short start, he followed, and as he left the inn the well-known smell of burning, aromatic herbs was in his nostrils. His wife was by now a few hundred yards away and had nearly cleared the little hamlet, heading for the open moor. As she proceeded a singular episode occurred. Mr Fowke thought little of it at the time, but much, later.

A sheep-dog was lying asleep by the roadside and as Mrs Fowke drew near it suddenly started up and, with back upraised and tail depressed, uttered a melancholy howl and darted through the hedge.

Mrs Fowke paid not the least attention to the dog, but pursued her way steadily through the rapidly falling dusk. Her husband followed as steadily, and thus for a long time they wound their way upwards towards the loneliest and wildest part of the Fells. It was by now night, but the moon had risen and flooded the landscape with her rays. The couple, one about two hundred yards behind the other, were now mounting the side of a steep hill, and hitherto Mr Fowke had remained in the pleasant belief that his presence was unsuspected by his wife. He was to be undeceived. The lady passed round a corner of the hill, thereby disappearing from sight; Mr Fowke hastened after her and on passing the corner in his turn found himself confronted by his wife, who stood watching for his appearance with a sarcastic smile.

She greeted him: 'Well, Mr Spy, are you very much puzzled?'

He remained silent, dumb with astonishment and chagrin, and she went on: 'I have been wondering what to do with you ever since you left home, but I have decided at last. You shall see all there is to see; I don't think you can do any harm and you may be useful by and by. Follow me.' And she turned and went on again.

Mr Fowke followed silently and abashed. Presently he became aware of a rosy light shining in front of them, and after walking a few yards more he found himself standing by the side of his wife on the edge of a small, cup-shaped hollow in the hills. In the centre of this hollow a large fire was burning and near the fire Mr Fowke could make out a pile of stones shaped like a rough altar. A group of about half a dozen people, all clad in the same grey, hooded cloaks, were sitting silently near the fire; and towards these his wife now began to descend, first telling him in a low, imperious voice to stay where he was. As Stella advanced down the declivity the group by the fire became aware of her approach, and rising, moved to meet her with gestures of greeting and respect. Stella passed through them, haughtily returning their salutations and slowly ascending the stone altar seated herself on a rock near its summit. As soon as she had taken up her position, she gave a signal, and the others forming round the fire commenced a slow and stately dance to the accompaniment of their own low chanting.

Mr Fowke watched absorbed. Gradually the dance grew quicker and wilder and the chanting louder, the whirling forms flung themselves into grotesque attitudes and shrieked ejaculations, the meaning of which Mr Fowke began dimly to divine though the words were strange. Suddenly they were silent and still and at the same moment Stella rose from her seat and, throwing back her hood and turning towards the summit of the altar, began in her turn to take up the chant. As she sang and bowed towards the topmost stone, her face and figure seemed transformed. In the flickering firelight and pale moon-shine she seemed to grow weirdly and horribly beautiful and to grow statelier and taller in her person. Slowly, too, as the song progressed the horrified watcher saw another change. A grey cloud formed on the summit of the altar, diminishing, thickening and turning into a Shape, a Shape of evil and fear. The silent group by the fire once more broke forth into wild gesticulations and cries, Stella prostrated herself, the Form on the altar grew clearer and with a cry of horror Mr Fowke turned away and rushed madly across the moor.

He never knew where he went or what he did. When he once more recovered his senses it was broad day and he was alone and lost on the moors. It was late afternoon before, broken and exhausted, he reached his own home, where the first person to greet him was his wife, cool and collected as ever. She led him into his study.

'Well,' she said, 'and what are you going to do now? Are you going to go about telling a cock-and-bull story of the moors, or are you going to be a good little man and hold your tongue? Don't imagine

I care,' she went on. 'The Great One can protect his servants and destroy his enemies.'

Mr Fowke groaned. 'It was true then,' he said, 'not a horrid dream.'

'You had better call it that,' she answered with a laugh and left him. Mr Fowke was utterly perplexed and, like many men of weak character, could decide on nothing. So matters drifted on: he had little or no communication with his wife, who was, however, invariably civil and pleasant when they met with a kind of mocking courtesy, which maddened him. At last came the day when she announced her intention of again going to I.

'And perhaps you would like to go with me,' she said. '*You* will be ready for the grey robe soon.'

She went and he spent the night in an agony of prayer.

The next day Stella returned and came immediately to his study. This time, however, she had no look of exhilaration on her face, she was troubled and angry. 'How dare you interfere with us,' she began, 'with your paltry little prayers and tears? You disturbed us last night. The Great One was angry – ' She stopped and then went on, 'I shall have to find a means of silencing you; it was a mistake to show you what I did.'

He looked at her. 'So it is not too late, is it?' he said. 'I can perhaps save you and drag you away from – '

She interrupted him. 'Silence,' she cried violently, 'or I will take steps to quiet you; I will blast you; I will call upon the Powers of the Air. I will – ' she was going on madly in her excitement when suddenly she became rigid, her face blanched and she fell senseless to the floor in a fit.

Mr Fowke raised the prostrate body, laid it on a sofa and summoned help. The unfortunate woman was carried to her bedroom, still unconscious, and the doctor sent for. He was an ordinary country practitioner and the case seemed to be clearly beyond his powers to deal with, but he emphasised the need of a trained nurse; and, one being fortunately available in the village, she was presently duly installed at the Parsonage.

After having seen all done that was possible, Mr Fowke, utterly worn out, retired to rest. Towards midnight he was awakened by a knocking at his door and opening it found the nurse pale and trembling on the threshold. She instantly assured him that she must throw up the case and leave the house at once. She could or would give no clear reasons for her action, but repeated again and again that she would sacrifice her whole professional career rather than remain in that sick room. Things had happened there, she said, things she could not tell of, but the place was accursed. In vain Mr Fowke tried to reassure her; she would not remain and so, bidding her go to her room till morning without disturbing the household, Mr Fowke went to his wife's room to take up the vigil himself.

When he entered the sick room all was still. Stella was lying motionless, breathing gently and at intervals murmuring a few words in her native tongue. Mr Fowke settled himself down in an armchair and gradually fell into a doze.

He woke suddenly as the clock struck three and glanced around him. The lamp had burnt low and the room was very cold. His wife still lay quietly in her bed, muttering softly to herself, but as Mr Fowke watched her, by the dim light, he fancied he noticed a horrible change in her. Gone were the full rounded outlines of a woman's form, the figure on the bed had become angular and mis-shaped. Her hand and arm, which lay outside the coverlet, were also changed and looked like a claw. Her face, too, was changing. As he watched, her beauty faded, the features altered, they ran together, became distorted, misplaced and, with a shudder, he found himself gazing on the lineaments of an unknown, hideous beast. Paralysed with horror he could not stir.

All at once there was a movement. The figure on the bed shivered violently, lifted itself up and sat gazing out beyond the foot of the bed. Mr Fowke followed the direction of its eyes and saw growing up slowly at the end of the room a grey, shapeless form, of which the burning eyes alone were distinct.

The creature on the bed moved and slipping back the bedclothes stepped suddenly to the floor. Mr Fowke saw that the lower limbs and, in fact, every part of it save the face that he could see were covered with a thick, grey fur. It moved again and passed swiftly across the room towards the grim shape in the corner; he heard its hoofs tap on the bare floor as it passed. It reached the motionless watcher, whose eyes seemed to blaze as it approached, and with a swift movement the two forms met, intermingled and – Mr Fowke could bear no more; he fainted.

It was daylight when he regained his senses. He glanced towards the bed; Mrs Fowke lay there calm, beautiful and dead.

The Picture

A superstition still exists in a certain part of Hungary that if a girl on New Year's Eve, after the performance of some simple ceremonies, looks into a darkened looking-glass, she will see reflected in it the face of her future husband, provided always that matrimony is destined to be her fate during the ensuing twelve months.

On a certain New Year's Eve not so very many years ago a group of village girls, who had assembled at the house of the farmer Ivan in company with their elders to welcome the New Year, were indulging in this ceremony amid peals of laughter and with apparently varying success. Amongst them was one Anna Pavlinski; when it came to her turn and she had looked in the glass she uttered a slight exclamation and laid the mirror down in some haste. No questioning by her companions elicited any information, but after the party had broken up she confided to her grandmother that she had distinctly seen the face of a man in the glass whom she did not know, but of whom she gave a very clear description.

When she had finished her grandmother sat for a short time in silence and then said: 'I do not understand it, Anna, but I charge you most earnestly to forget what you have seen. You have described clearly a man whom I have known; it was many years ago and if he is indeed still alive he must be absolutely different now from this vision you have seen. But I believe him to be dead and that his evil soul is where he can no longer work mischief. Never speak or think of him again. No good can come of it.'

Whether Anna followed the advice of her grandmother in every respect is not known, but at any rate she never spoke again of her vision.

* * *

It is now necessary to introduce the characters of the story, and I begin with the heroine, Anna Pavlinski, the eighteen-year-old daughter of the bailiff of the W. property in Hungary. Her grand-father had been a man who by his own talents had raised himself to a position superior to that of the majority of the peasantry, and at the time of his death had been what corresponds in England to the foreman carpenter on the estate of the Counts of W. In 1848 when, as is well known, there were revolutionary disturbances in various parts of Hungary, he had been the leader of a mob which had attacked the castle of W.

The object of the mob had been somewhat indefinite, but it had shown a desire to get hold of and probably to kill the then Count W. This gentleman, however, had not been found in the castle and the mob had dispersed without doing serious harm. In fact, except for a looting of the wine-cellars and the chasing away of a few Austrian servants who formed the Count's household and who fled the neigh-bourhood in fear of their lives, no harm was done. After the troubles, which were not serious in this part of the country, for some reason this Pavlinska was not arrested and found himself left undisturbed in his position of foreman carpenter.

About four years after the rising Pavlinski was at work one day executing repairs to the roof of the castle when, according to the testimony of a fellow workman, he suddenly threw up his arm, as if to ward off a blow, uttered an unintelligible cry and staggering back-wards fell into the courtyard below, where he was picked up with a broken neck. At the time of his death Pavlinska was married and had one child, a son to whom he had given a good education, and as he was endowed with some natural abilities, the young man gradually rose to a position equivalent to that of estate bailiff.

Some years after his father's death, the younger Pavlinski returned one day from a tour of the property and, having dismounted, was standing by his horse in the courtyard of the castle, when the animal suddenly became terrified and lashing out kicked his master on the head, causing instant death. It was noticed at the time that the horse became tranquil again after the tragedy as suddenly as it had become excited. Pavlinski the younger had also married and at the time of his death was a widower with one daughter, Anna, a girl of about fifteen years of age, whose mother had died at the time of her birth. She and her grandmother were, therefore, the only surviving members of the Pavlinski family and, being left in poor circum-stances, they took up their abode with a distant relative of the elder woman, a well-to-do farmer named Ivan. Under his roof Anna lived up to the age of eighteen, making herself useful to her host and hostess and receiving, through the care of her grandmother, a slightly superior education to most of the village girls. She developed into a good-looking lass of a rather reserved and dreamy temperament, full of imagination, and was not especially popular with the young people of the village since they felt that she was in a sense aloof from and different to themselves.

Count W.'s castle, the scene of the tragic events connected with the Pavlinski family, was a large and handsome building standing on a slight eminence to the west of the village. The entrance hall and other parts of the castle situated on its eastern side were of great antiquity and looked down on to it from a distance of about half a mile; the western part of the castle was of more modern construction and commanded an extensive view of the Hungarian plain.

In 1848 the direct line of the W. family had dwindled down to one representative, who was popularly known locally as 'the wicked Count'. His reputation, however, was largely one of hearsay as far as the village was concerned and was founded chiefly on the fact that, contrary to Hungarian traditions, he had embraced in his youth the side of the Austrian Government, had gone to Vienna and had there joined the Imperial Guard. After some years' service in the Austrian Army he had retired, and after a further stay in the metropolis had returned to W. where he lived a quiet life attended exclusively by imported Austrian servants.

His means were scanty, as the estate was much decayed and it was by no means clear whence he derived income sufficient to maintain himself at all. He was addicted to sudden and secret comings and goings and popular rumour ascribed to him the part of an Austrian secret agent, hence his local sobriquet.

In appearance Count W. was a tall, handsome man with curly dark hair and black eyes, and in 1848 was about forty-five years old. At the time of the *émeute* previously described he was residing at the castle, and it was greatly to the astonishment of the mob that he was not found therein, but presumably he had had warning of their coming and had escaped. What was even more singular was that he never reappeared. After that autumn afternoon in 1848 he vanished completely and some years later, his death being presumed, the estate passed to a distant relative then living in America. This gentleman did not care to leave his American interests in order to take possession of a practically bankrupt estate and accordingly selected a firm of agents in Budapest to take charge of his affairs, closed up the castle and caused caretakers to be established therein, pending the date when he might wish actually to reside in his Hungarian home. Such was the position of the castle of W. at the date of the opening of the story.

Two or three months had elapsed since the scene first described when one day old Michael, the custodian of the castle, hobbled down to Ivan's home, which stood at the entrance to the village, in considerable distress. He himself had long been crippled with rheumatism and the bulk of the work at the castle had been performed by his old wife. He now came to explain that she had fallen down and injured her hip and that he was anxious to obtain the help of one of the village girls to look after his wife and to do what was necessary at the castle.

After some talk it was arranged that Anna should go to the help of Michael and his wife, and it was not long before she found herself installed in her new work. At first it was expected that the old woman would soon recover; but she did not do so, and Anna quickly became so indispensable that at the next visit of the Budapest agent Michael pleaded for her permanent appointment. This was arranged without undue difficulty.

Anna now became a regular resident of the castle and found plenty to occupy her in looking after the old couple and in doing a certain amount of airing and cleaning in its closed up rooms. She also began for the first time to keep a diary of her daily life, and it is upon this diary that we depend for the next portion of the story.

Matters appear to have gone on quite uneventfully until midsummer, when on the eve of the Feast of St John Anna found herself engaged in cleaning in the West Gallery, a long and noble apartment in the newer part of the castle. She had actually finished her day's work and before going downstairs was standing by the last open window leaning against the framework and gazing dreamily out over the low Hungarian plain toward the setting sun. All was absolutely still, no air was stirring and the only sounds audible were the noises of a distant farmyard. She was about to close the window and leave the gallery, when she was startled by hearing a low sigh behind her followed by a. gentle rustle. She turned hastily, to see nothing to account for the sigh, but the rustle was easily explained by the slipping off of the covering of one of the pictures behind her. The rays of the setting sun shone full upon it and showed it to be the portrait of a tall, dark, handsome man of about forty years of age, clothed in the fashion of some thirty-five years previously.

In an instant Anna recognised the picture as being that of the visionary being she had seen in the looking glass, of which the memory had never left her. Rapt in astonishment, Anna moved nearer the picture and saw by the legend on the frame that it was the portrait of the so-called 'wicked Count W.' who had vanished mysteriously so many years ago. She gazed fixedly at the picture and as the declining beams of the sun shed their last glory upon it, it seemed to her that human intelligence showed itself in its painted lines; the features seemed to become endued with life and to smile upon her. As she stood before it an awful sense of an un-folding mystery took possession of her, she was filled with joy, joy at the manifestation vouchsafed to her; she was filled with fear, fear of the uncanny, of the unknown future that was spreading itself before her. At that moment she heard Michael's voice calling from below and, hastily shutting the window, she ran down-stairs. Neither then nor at any subsequent time did she speak of her experience either to Michael or to her grandmother, nor did she follow her general household instructions and replace the cover-ing on the picture, which gradually came to exercise an extraordinary fascination upon her. It became her habit to spend long hours gazing at and, as she imagined, communing with it, in fact her diary is filled to a large extent with her accounts of mystic correspond-ence with her painted lover, for into such she gradually trans-formed the picture.

Time went on until one afternoon in September when old Michael once more came down to Ivan's home in as great trouble as before, this time to report the disappearance of Anna. It appeared from his story that her work that day had consisted in cleaning out a room known as the Countess's boudoir, which adjoined the West Gallery. The last time she had been seen was at about half-past three, when she had come downstairs in search of some article needed for her work. She was then in her usual health and spirits and, having found what she sought, had returned to her work. She usually came down to the lower floor, where she and the caretakers lived, at five to attend to various small duties, and since at half-past five o'clock she had not appeared Michael had called to her and receiving no reply had gone upstairs to seek for her. He found the Countess's boudoir littered with Anna's household implements but no trace of the girl, for whom he consequently made search elsewhere.

In the course of this search he discovered the uncovered picture of the wicked Count and an open window in the West Gallery, but of Anna he could see and hear nothing. Although his wife was positive that Anna had not gone out, he decided ultimately to go down to Ivan's home, partly in the faint hope of finding her there and partly to give the alarm and obtain help for a further and more thorough investigation of the castle. Ivan and one of his sons accordingly returned there with the old man, but despite a careful search in all parts of the building they could find nothing to indicate what had become of Anna. The following day another search party, headed by the village priest, made an even more careful exploration of the castle and its surroundings, but with like result. Anna had vanished as mysteriously as the Count and, like him, she never reappeared. The affair created a village sensation but was forgotten, save by a few, after the lapse of some years.

Some eight years after the disappearance of Anna the then owner of the property wrote to his Budapest agents that, having made a fortune sufficient for his needs, he intended to leave America and take up his abode at W. He gave instructions that the castle should be put in repair and modern conveniences installed.

A firm of Budapest builders was employed for the purpose, and in the course of their work the following curious discoveries were made. In the eastern or older part of the castle was situated the great entrance hall panelled with magnificent old oak. It was necessary to remove part of this panelling temporarily, and the workmen engaged on the task discovered close to the entrance to the castle a movable panel in the woodwork, which formed the outside of a strong secret door. This door opened on to a short passage leading into a tiny but lofty room lighted and aired by a narrow slit in the stonework above the main entrance. In this room were a chair and a small table, and seated at the table, with its arm resting on a bundle of papers, was a skeleton which by the remains of the dress was easily identifiable as that of the missing Count. The papers proved that he had been in the secret employ of the Austrian police, and it seems clear that on learning of the approach of the mob he had fled for safety to this hiding-place, taking the papers with him. It was noted, however, that the spring opening the door from within was broken, and it was therefore evident that once the Count had entered the passage and closed the door he was a prisoner.

Whether he knew that the lock was hampered, and relied on being able to summon aid by calling his servants after the mob had gone, or whether he himself broke the spring in attempting to open the door cannot now be known, but it will be remembered that the mob drove the servants away from the castle, which remained absolutely deserted for a period more than long enough to cause the Count's death by starvation. He had evidently met his fate with resignation and had died in his chair with his arm on his papers. *His* fate forms no great mystery, but the discovery of a second skeleton in the little room gives rise to a more interesting problem. For, crouching at the foot of the Count in a kneeling position and in an attitude of adoration, was found the skeleton of a girl which it was not difficult to identify as that of the lost Anna.

The problem to solve is: how did she reach the place where she was found, why was she found in that attitude, and why did she not permit herself to be rescued by the searchers?

At the time of the discovery Anna's grandmother, Michael and his wife were all dead, but the priest and Ivan were both alive and narrated the happenings of that September afternoon to the Budapest agent who, summoned in haste, came to W. and saw the bodies in the position in which they were found.

It was clear that at half-past three on the afternoon of her disappearance Anna was in good health and spirits. Her diary showed that up to the night before she had been ignorant of the existence of the secret room; it is impossible that she should have known it and of its contents and should not have mentioned them in her diary. As she did not come down to the kitchen at five o'clock it must be assumed that at some time between half-past three and five o'clock something occurred which caused her to leave her work in one part of the castle, go to another part, discover a secret room and voluntarily shut herself up in it – it was proved that the door of the secret passage was not self-closing.

And having entered the secret room why did she kneel down and adore a skeleton? Most people, young girls especially, on finding themselves in such company would have done their best to escape from it; again, why did she not make her presence in the secret room known to one or other of the search parties? It is unlikely that she died so quickly as not to have heard either Michael or later on the first search party calling in the East Hall, though it is possible she may have succumbed before the advent of the priest's party on the following day. The questions, as my friend, the Budapest agent, said, are easy enough to put but impossible to answer unless one is willing to believe that the wicked Count, driven to his terrible death by the mob headed by Pavlinski, continued after leaving his earthly body to pursue Pavlinski and his family with his vengeance. The seemingly accidental and violent deaths within the walls of the castle of the two male members of the family may perhaps be thus explained, as well as the singular illusions which lured to her end the unfortunate Anna, the last of her race.

The Governess's Story

We were sitting, a large group of us, round the blazing fire in the old hall one Christmas Eve and the conversation, guided by both hour and place, drifted on to things supernatural. Among those present was old Miss Hosmer, a lady well-known and popular, who, after an early life of struggle and poverty, was now spending her declining years in comfort on a modest fortune, derived from the bequest of a distant relative. In her youth Miss Hosmer had earned her livelihood as a governess and in the course of her scholastic career she had lived in various families and had undergone various experiences, some grave, some, but alas fewer, gay; she had seen the skeletons kept in more than one cupboard and had been the confidante of more than one curious story.

As a rule she was chary of recounting her experiences, since she rightly held that the histories of others, however discovered, should be kept confidential, and that more mischief is the result of idle gossip than comes from malicious tale-bearing. In person, she was small, grey-haired, old-fashioned, with a keen sense of humour twinkling in her blue eyes and a warm corner in her heart for those in difficulty or distress. During the early part of our talk, she had remained silent, listening with a queer expression of detachment to the various stories that circulated round the circle, and contributing nothing to them till directly appealed to by Mrs Leveson, one of her former and well-loved pupils.

In a pause of the conversation, Mrs Leveson turned abruptly to Miss Hosmer and said: 'Can't you tell us a story, Miss Hosmer? I know you have told me more than once that when you were quite a young woman you saw a ghost.'

'No, my dear,' answered Miss Hosmer, 'I never told you that. I never saw a ghost in all my life.'

'But surely you had some queer experience of that nature, didn't you?' returned Mrs Leveson.

'Well,' said the other, 'I did once have an adventure of the sort you mention. I don't often speak of it nowadays, and I try to think of it as little as I can.'

'Why?' I interrupted, 'Is it anything so very dreadful?'

'No,' said Miss Hosmer slowly. 'It was not really dreadful, but it was very, very sad, and I feel, perhaps, that I should be doing harm and causing pain to perfectly innocent people by repeating it.'

'But not if you conceal the names and places,' answered Mr Davies, the barrister, 'and, now you have roused our curiosity so much, surely you will gratify it and tell us the story.'

Miss Hosmer hesitated for a few minutes, and then replied: 'Well, perhaps you are right and, in any case, I hope and believe that I can so conceal identities that none of you will know of whom I am speaking. But I beg,' she went on, 'that if any of you do guess, you will keep your guesses to yourselves. Two of the people implicated are alive today, and I would not for the world that either of them should have the slightest inkling of what happened in their family when they were little children.'

We promised as she desired, and Miss Hosmer began.

'What I am going to tell you is an experience that I actually underwent many years ago, when I was quite a girl, and had only recently taken up governessing as a means of earning my daily bread. I had been out of a situation for some little time, and was beginning to grow anxious as to my future; so that it was with a feeling of real happiness that one morning I opened a letter from Miss Butler, at whose agency I was registered, in which she asked me to come round to her office as soon as possible. It was not long before I was with her, when she told me that she had just had an application from Lady K., the widow of the late Sir Arthur K., G.C.M.G., for a young lady to come to her in the country to educate her two children, a boy of nine and a little girl of seven, and to give especial attention to preparing the boy for school. Up to the present, so far as I could gather, Lady K. had had entire charge of the education of the children since her husband's death, but she did not feel herself capable of instructing the boy sufficiently to prepare him for school, and she also desired a resident governess to continue the girl's education after the boy had left home.

'Miss Butler gave me Lady K.'s letter to read, and I gleaned from it that the family resided always at the family seat Wyke Hall, near the town of Dellingham, in one of the Midland Counties. The work appeared to be exactly what I wanted and felt capable of undertaking; the terms offered were quite satisfactory, and the quietness of the life was by no means distasteful to me, since I have always been a lover of the country. It was accordingly arranged that I should write to Lady K. and seek an interview with her to go further into the matter. I returned to my rooms without delay and, having written and posted my letter, I hunted up an old book of reference that had belonged to my father to see what mention it made of the K. family. I quickly found what I sought and learned that Sir Arthur K. had died in 1887, leaving three children. He had been twice married, once to a Miss C. in 1874, by whom he had had one son, Edward, born in 1877, and again in 1883 to a Miss Constance G. by whom he had had two children, Arthur, born in 1884, and Eleanor, born in 1886. As the year of which I am speaking was 1893, this would make the ages of the three children sixteen, nine, and seven respectively. Except that the family residence was Wyke Hall, which I knew already, this was all the information my rather out-of-date reference book contained about the K. family.

'In course of post I received a reply from Lady K. stating that she would be at a certain hotel in London, on a certain not distant date, and asking me to call and see her there. I complied with her request, and one fine morning late in August, 1893, beheld me ushered in a rather nervous condition into the presence of Lady K. On entering the private sitting-room where she was awaiting me, as she rose from her chair to greet me I saw before me a tall, stately, handsome woman of about thirty-five years of age. She was a blonde with aquiline features, a handsome, well-preserved figure, dressed in handsome though rather old-fashioned clothes. Her voice was gentle, low and cold, with a curiously monotonous intonation. Her manners were dignified and reserved, though perfectly courteous. She was in half-mourning, and wore no jewellery.

'In short, a first glance displayed a rather fine, if cold-looking woman of the world; a closer inspection revealed something else. Beneath all her perfect manners and frigid exterior there seethed a medley of strong passions; and among these, lurking in the depths and only occasionally peeping forth, was fear. I have always been something of a physiognomist, and I felt sure I was not deceived. Of what she was in fear, and of what was concealed beneath that calm exterior, I could not even hazard a guess; but that Lady K. possessed a secret, and a painful if not a terrible one, I was not an instant in doubt. After our formal greetings we stood looking at each other, and in that brief moment I formed the conviction that I did not and never could like Lady K. However, it is not for a hard-up governess to pick and choose. If Lady K. liked me, I felt I was bound to accept her situation; it would have been impossible for me to go back to Miss Butler and tell her that I had refused an excellent position with a family of standing, simply because I did not like an indescribable something in my would-be employer's face,

'Well, I need not go into the details of my interview with Lady K. except to say that she made most particular and minute enquiries into my capabilities, qualities, failings, good points, family and, in fact, every conceivable thing about me. My sense of dislike to her was not intensified by this inquisition, in fact it rather raised her in my opinion as being evidence that she was a careful and conscientious woman. I noticed also that the mention of her children was the sole thing that brought a gleam of light and happiness into that cold, hard face.

Evidently she adored her little Arthur, her little Eleanor. After a long interview we parted, I going out with the assurance of Lady K. that, if the references with which I had supplied her were as satisfactory as our conversation, I might consider myself engaged to come to Wyke Hall after the holidays were over – in about a month's time.

'The references proved satisfactory, and one evening in late September saw me arriving at Dellingham Station. It was a fine evening, but the journey from town had been long and tedious and it was growing dark by the time I left the station. Outside, I found awaiting me a well-appointed, single-horse brougham, driven by a neatly liveried and respectful groom. Into this I mounted and my luggage having been bestowed on the carriage rack we started off for Wyke Hall. So far as I could see, after we had disengaged ourselves from the streets of the little town of Dellingham, we drove through a typical English midland county landscape; gentle rolling hills, green pasture and well-kept arable land were intermingled, and our road seemed to follow generally the course of the little river Dell. We passed smiling farmhouses and pleasant cottages during the drive: our lines lay in peaceful and homelike places. About five miles from Dellingham, so far as I could judge, the brougham turned up an elm-shaded avenue, and in a few minutes more stopped before the door of

Wyke Hall. It was now almost dark, and I could see but little of the house, except that it appeared to be of fair size and to be surrounded by a broad, stone-flagged terrace.

'The front door was opened by a neat-looking footman in livery, behind whom loomed the more dignified form of a middle-aged butler, and I entered the hall, which was of considerable size. Opposite the front door was another, which led into Lady K.'s private sitting and business room. Close to this second door, the main staircase of the house commenced; this led up to a wide gallery on the first floor. Out of this gallery on the left-hand side opened a swing-door which gave access to the upper passage of the wing. The butler, having relieved me of my handbag and umbrella, led the way across the hall and ushered me into Lady K.'s room.

'Lady K. greeted me with as much cordiality as she appeared capable of assuming, seated me by the fire, ordered me up a belated, but much welcome tea, enquired about my journey and generally did her best to give me a polite welcome. I still, however, could not get over that faint sense of dislike towards her, which I had felt from the first, and it was with relief that I heard her say as I put down my tea cup: "Well, now I suppose you would like to meet the children. I will send for them to come down."

'And in a few minutes down they came, and at once I fell in love with both of them. It has been my lot to teach and to love many young people, but, assuredly, I can say that in all my experience I never met two to whom I took so quick and warm a fancy, and from whom I received so soon such affectionate devotion. Of the two, perhaps my favourite was the boy, Arthur; he was fair like his mother, but instead of her cold expression he was bubbling over with life and good spirits. He was the leader of the two, and ruled his little sister with a vigour, which, if it had not been loving, would have been merciless. She reciprocated his devotion, and was never so happy as when trotting after him and carrying out his instructions. She was dark – I presume she took after her father – and intelligent, but Arthur was an unusually brilliant child.

We spent a little time in making acquaintance, and I became confirmed in my original opinion that the one really soft spot in Lady K. was her passionate adoration of her children.

'After about half an hour thus spent, Lady K. rose and said she was sure I would wish to see my own quarters, and we accordingly all of us proceeded upstairs. On reaching the swing-door on the upper floor Lady K. pushed it open, and descending a couple of steps we entered the wing of the house, which was traversed by a wide but not lengthy passage terminating in a large window. Lady K. threw open the first door on the right hand of this passage and disclosed a large, cheerful-looking room, the schoolroom and general living room, in which the children spent the bulk of their waking hours. Having duly inspected this apartment, we proceeded down the passage to the door of a second room which formed the end room of the house.

This was my bedroom, and I confess to a feeling of surprise and pleasure at seeing the bright and pretty room, a cheerful fire blazing in the grate, a vase of autumn flowers on the dressing-table, and books and knick-knacks scattered round.

'After a brief pause we returned to the main part of the house, Lady K. explaining that the room opposite mine was an unused spare bedroom, whilst the space opposite the schoolroom was occupied by a bathroom, housemaids' closet and similar small offices. On entering the main hall, Lady K. pointed out her bedroom, which adjoined the schoolroom, and was situated above the room downstairs into which I had first been shown. In this, she explained, Eleanor slept with her, whilst Arthur's bedroom was the adjoining one, and had formerly been her husband's dressing-room. Beyond these rooms I could see the vista of the main passage through the body of the mansion, but my story does not concern itself with any other than the part of the house I have described, save that I should mention that shortly beyond Arthur's room I saw the bottom of the staircase leading up to the servants' attics overhead.

'Our inspection of the house concluded, Lady K. suggested that I should probably wish to retire to my room to unpack and rest, and departed downstairs, taking the children with her.

'I went back to my bedroom, where my luggage, unstrapped and prepared for unpacking, stood neatly ranged, and sat down to think over the events of the last hour. My thoughts should have been pleasant. Here I was welcomed with the utmost courtesy, my future pupils appeared charming and lovable, my surroundings were most comfortable and my convenience had been thoughtfully studied. I should mention that before the children had come down Lady K. had outlined her ideas as to hours of study and recreation, subject to my approval, and had arranged that I should breakfast and have tea with the children in the schoolroom, lunch with her and them downstairs, and that after they had retired for the night I should be served with my evening meal upstairs, so that I might have my entire evenings free and to myself. These plans suited me perfectly; all seemed rose-coloured, and yet I could not dispel a lurking feeling of ill-ease for which I could not account. On the whole I felt that it centred round the personality of Lady K. Nothing could be more civil than her manner, nothing could excel her apparent kindness, but – I could not complete my thought, and whilst I was still dreaming there came a tap at the door and an old woman, evidently a confidential upper servant, entered. She at once introduced herself as Mason, whom I had heard mentioned as Lady K.'s personal maid and hitherto the attendant on the children as well. She was a quiet, self-effaced woman, grey-haired, blue eyed, and with a sad but not unpleasing face. She explained that she had ventured to come to see if I needed any help, but I suspected that her real motive was to get an early inspection of me, her supplanter with the children. However, I had no wish not to be friendly, and begged her to sit down. She took a chair, and we very quickly found ourselves in friendly talk; she was eloquent on the subject of both the children, but especially of Arthur, and I gleaned a good deal of information from her about their ways and characters. All I heard was satisfactory, but I observed that once or twice when I endeavoured to turn the conversation in the direction of Lady K. Mason immediately became uncommunicative, and swung the talk back on to the merits of the young people. Our chat lasted perhaps half an hour, when Mason departed to assist Lady K. at her evening toilet, and shortly after a neat, smiling maidservant, who informed me that she was the schoolroom-maid, knocked at my door with the intelligence that my evening meal was ready in the schoolroom.

'Supper finished, I sat awhile still trying to analyse my thoughts and, not succeeding, I returned to my bedroom where I busied myself with my unpacking until feeling rather tired I desisted and went to bed.

'It was not long, I think, before I fell asleep and slept soundly till I was gradually awakened at what I afterwards ascertained was about half-past eleven by the sound of someone walking about in the room above mine. At first the footsteps seemed to mingle with my dreams, but as my senses became clearer the sounds also became more distinct. They were the footsteps of someone walking hastily and irregularly: at times they fell slowly or stopped, at others they hurried almost into a run. They moved all about the room, not confining themselves to any single path or beat, and, though clear and distinct, were not heavy. I remember wondering at the sex of the walker: the steps sounded too light for those of a man and too long for those of a woman. A slight sense of annoyance passed over me; surely it was very late for a servant to be up, and very improper for one of the apparently highly trained domestics of Wyke Hall to be indulging in such antics. Suddenly I heard a window in the room above thrown wide open with a crash and then followed absolute silence. The steps had ceased, and in a little while I fell asleep to wake the next morning to pouring rain.

'The day was a hopeless one and going out was not to be thought of. Accordingly, after we had finished our first morning's school-room work, at which I was delighted with the manners and attitude of both my pupils, Lady K., who had come in more than once to watch our progress, suggested a game in the billiard-room. This room proved to be in the space below the schoolroom and my bedroom, and the game was a great treat to the children, since they explained they were never allowed to play about on the billiard table by themselves, and that Lady K. hardly ever used to indulge them by rushing about after the balls. The rest of the day passed without incident, and I retired to rest feeling myself gradually becoming at home and inclined to laugh at my uncomfortable feelings of the evening before.

'I suppose it was the lack of exercise, but I did not fall asleep as promptly as is my usual custom and, as I lay wakeful, all at once I heard the footsteps in the room above. They began absolutely without warning, and as on the previous night moved irregularly about the room, now fast, now slow. I looked at my watch: it was a little after half-past eleven. As on the previous night, I heard the window thrown violently open, and then came silence. I slept after a while undisturbed and woke in the morning with one of my trying sick headaches.

'It was a prostrating one, but I had my duty to attend to, and I got through the morning somehow, but when Lady K. came into the schoolroom, towards the end of the lesson I saw her eye me sharply and, I thought, uneasily.

' "Are you not well, Miss Hosmer?" she said.

' "I have only got a tiresome headache," I replied. "I am afraid I am rather subject to them, and I expect it was not getting out yesterday, and sleeping badly brought it on, but it will soon pass off."

' "Did you not sleep well?" queried Lady K. with, I thought, a trace of excitement and anxiety in her voice. She hesitated an instant and went on, "I hope nothing disturbed you."

'Yes, there was no doubt – there was anxiety in that last sentence. At the moment the thought of the steps had faded from my mind: as a matter of fact, they had not really disturbed me the night before, or been the cause of my headache.

' "I did not sleep well," I replied, "but it was my headache coming on; my room and bed are most comfortable."

'Lady K. looked relieved. "Well, you must be quiet now," she said. "I will take the children out and you must rest and get your head better."

'I followed her instructions, lay down, and my headache was so far recovered that I was able to come down to luncheon and go on with the day's programme in the afternoon. This involved an out-of-door excursion, in the shape of a walk; the children lamented the rule, as they wanted to take me round the gardens and stables to exhibit their various treasures, but Lady K. had laid down a strict rule. "A walk in the afternoon, playing in the garden in the morning", and Lady K. was not one to disobey. So we explored the surrounding Park, and got various views of the house, which showed itself as a finer and larger place than my first nocturnal glimpse had led me to believe. That night the exhaustion following my headache soon put me to sleep, and if the restless domestic walked above me my ears were closed to his or her footsteps.

'The next day broke quiet and uneventful. I felt quite settled down now, my affection for the children grew steadily, and I think they reciprocated it; the servants including Mason were civil and accommodating, and even my subconscious feeling about Lady K. was beginning to diminish. But my peace of mind was to receive a shock that day, and that shock came through the innocent instrumentality of my pupils. We had been rambling about the gardens and stables and farmyard, and I had made the acquaintance of Galloper and Queenie, the two ponies, of the carriage horses, of the big Newfoundland Steady, and of the stable terrier Spot. I had duly admired the two little plots dignified by the names of Master Arthur's and Miss Eleanor's gardens. I had looked at the pigs and at the poultry, and had gazed from afar upon those more formidable creatures, the cows, and we were now returning home rather hastily, for the lunch hour was close upon us, when an argument arose between the two children, as to the proper allocation of the windows in the façade of the house, Eleanor maintaining and Arthur stoutly disputing as to which exactly were the windows of the schoolroom. Finally I was called upon to umpire the question, and, glancing at the windows in question, I was easily able to give my decision. But as I looked at the house, and at my windows adjoining those in dispute, I had a curious feeling of something being wrong. For a moment I was at a loss, and then it suddenly flashed across me: there were attics over the main body of the house, but the schoolroom and my bedroom were in the wing, and there were no attics above them. Where, then, could be the room above mine in which someone walked at night, and opened the window? A queer uncanny sensation passed over me, but I had no time to think the matter out, for we had reached the house and the luncheon bell was ringing.

'At luncheon Lady K. proposed that the afternoon should be devoted to driving into Dellingham to endeavour to acquire certain books, which I had asked for as necessary for my pupils, and I had accordingly no further opportunity to investigate the problem of the footsteps. That evening, though I was rather tired, I must confess that, after the schoolroom maid had removed my supper things and left me alone in the wing of the house, I felt just a trifle nervous and wakeful. However, I got resolutely to bed, and, leaving my candle alight, waited. The expected happened. Just after half-past eleven, without the slightest warning, the steps recommenced their restless pacing. I had nerved myself as to what to do, and I instantly got out of bed and, slipping on my dressing-gown, went out into the passage and closed my door. As soon as I had done so the sound of the footsteps diminished greatly; I went on into the schoolroom and here I could no longer hear them at all. I returned to the passage and, bracing up my courage, opened the door of the spare room. In this room, also, the steps were inaudible; I went back to my bedroom and again they rang out clear and distinct, and in a few minutes more I heard the window thrown up and all became silent. It was clear, therefore, that whatever caused the sound must be directly over my head. I lay awake that night for some time, absorbed in the problem; so far I was puzzled, and slightly nervous, but not exactly frightened. I did not believe in spiritual manifestations, and was convinced that some physical cause was the explanation of the mysterious sounds. At the same time I was sufficiently disturbed in mind to feel that I must discover this cause, or else that I should fall a prey to my nervous imagination. Ultimately I decided on taking the opportunity of the upper part of the house being empty during the servants' dinner hour, and of the children's half an hour with Lady K. after our luncheon, to make an exploration of the top storey of the mansion. So resolving, I fell asleep.

'The following day I ran briskly upstairs as soon as lunch was finished; the upper floors were deserted as I anticipated, and I made my way undisturbed to the attics. Here, I found the same long passage as below, save for the notable difference that in place of the swing-door opening into the wing there was a closed archway which appeared as if a door had existed there at one time and had been closed up, and instead there was a window in this archway, which gave light to that end of the passage. I approached the window, and opening it looked out. Beneath me, there was nothing except two low gables with a gutter between them which stretched away towards the end of the wing. One of these gables was clearly over my room and the schoolroom, the other over the rooms on the opposite side of the wing passage. A moment's inspection showed clearly enough that it was absolutely impossible for any room to exist within these gables, which could not have been above four feet high at their topmost point. I leaned out of the window for closer inspection, and suddenly noticed with something of a shock that both the roof and the end wall of the house appeared new, not above a few years old at most. Greatly puzzled, I drew back and tried the door of the attic above Lady K.'s room. It opened easily, and disclosed a room littered with boxes, disused furniture and other lumber. The room was so filled that it would have been impossible for anyone to have paced about it in the fashion I have described; the window also showed no signs of having been opened for a considerable time. Opposite this room was the empty space of the main hall, which extended clear up through the house. I was now greatly puzzled, and, I think, beginning to grow frightened. Who was the walker by night, and where did he walk?

'I had no further time to consider the question as I was compelled to return to my charges, but I decided to take Mason into my confidence and see if she could throw light upon the problem. That afternoon we sallied forth on our usual walk, and this time the children who were my eager guides led me in a new direction. The path which we traversed led us near Wyke churchyard, and we wandered into it to get a nearer view of the quaint old church. As we walked round the outside of the church, Arthur suddenly pulled my arm gently and pointing to a vault a few yards away said: "That's where Papa is buried, and poor Brother Edward too."

'The words gave me a start. I knew, of course, that Sir Arthur was dead, and probably buried in the neighbourhood of Wyke, but it had never occurred to me to think that his eldest son should be lying beside him. It is true that I had never up to this moment heard his name mentioned, but I had scarcely thought of him at all; I had supposed him away at school; I had never conceived the possibility of his being dead.

'It has always been my fixed rule never to try and obtain information as to their family affairs from my pupils, but in this instance I could not restrain myself from the question: "I did not know your brother was dead. When did it happen?"

' "Oh, a long time ago," said Arthur. "Eleanor cannot even remember him, but I can."

' "I remember him too," said Eleanor.

' "Yes, but you were too little to play with him like I did," said her brother.

'I did not like to press the discussion and the conversation came to an end; but I was more determined than ever to have a talk with old Mason. That evening I was doomed to disappointment, however, for on asking the schoolroom maid if Mason was in her room I was told that she had gone to stay the night with her brother, a tradesman in Dellingham.

'That night I lay awake and listened for the coming of the steps with a haunting sense of fear. There seemed to be no human agency accountable for them; was there some superhuman cause? Had I felt more at my ease with Lady K. I think I should have spoken to her, but there seemed to be some bar between us, which forbade any but formal intercourse. And in some way which I cannot define it was borne in upon me that she understood those steps, that in her hands lay the key of the mystery.

'The evening hours passed on, and at the appointed time the steps overhead once more sounded. My nerves had reached such a pitch of excitement that I felt I could have faced anything rather than remain in ignorance of their meaning. Had it been possible for me to have transported myself bodily to whatever place the walker moved in, I verily believe I should have rushed thither to face the unknown, to discover the secret. But it was impossible. I felt that night too terrified to leave my bed for the quiet of the schoolroom and, paradoxical as it seems, though I would have faced a ghost or an evil spirit in the unseen, unknown room above me, I could not face the well-known, quiet passage outside my door. The sounds above me ran their usual course, the steps ceased, the window was flung open, silence ensued and I finally forgot myself in an uneasy sleep.

'I woke the next morning nervous and unrefreshed; at lunch-time my state of nervousness was increased by my becoming painfully conscious of the fact that Lady K. was watching me covertly, gloomily, and withal with a certain indefinable expression as of one who expects and awaits a disaster. She talked nothing but commonplaces as usual, and I began to feel more and more confident that in her hands lay the key of the mystery of the night walker. Towards the end of luncheon Lady K. observed that as it was Saturday she thought the children might enjoy a ride. This suggestion was eagerly embraced by both of them, and I found myself with the whole afternoon free before me.

'In due course after luncheon, the ponies were announced to be ready, and having seen my charges safely started off in the highest spirits, under the care of a fatherly-looking old coachman, I mounted the stairs, and went directly to Mason's room, which was a small one in the main body of the house not far removed from Lady K's. own bedroom.

'When I entered Mason's room in answer to her "Come in", I fancied that for a moment she looked slightly discomposed, and as if my visit was not over welcome. However, she greeted me civilly, begged me to be seated, and, taking up her needle, resumed her sewing. For a moment there was silence, and then she began to ask questions about the children and their lessons in a vague and preoccupied way, as if solely for the purpose of making conversation and avoiding a disagreeable topic. I answered her as briefly as in courtesy I could do, and then plunged at once into my subject: "Mason, who is it that walks about every night over my head?"

'I paused and looked at her. She slowly laid down her work and, paling steadily till she grew a deathly white, sat staring at me in silence.

' "I cannot understand it," I went on, "What does it mean?"

'She seemed to find her voice with an effort. "I don't know what you are talking about, miss," she said. "There is nobody walks about this house at night."

' "I did not say that," I answered. "But there is someone who walks about over my head every night about half-past eleven and then throws open a window loud enough for anyone in the house to hear him."

' "Throws open the window," whispered Mason to herself, "Oh, my God! my God!" Then in a louder tone she went on, "You must be mistaken, miss, there is no room above yours."

' "That makes it all the stranger," I answered. "I know there is no room there, and yet I know the steps are there and nowhere else. What is it, oh, tell me what it is!"

'The strangeness of the episode, the old woman's obvious fear were telling on me; I felt I was losing my self-control, was giving way to panic. By a great effort, I regained my composure, and looking steadily at her said: "Mason, there is a story, a dreadful story connected with what I have heard at night. You know it, and you must tell it to me, or I shall go straight to Lady K. and ask her to tell me."

' "For the love of God do not do that, miss," cried Mason.

' "Very well then, tell me the story," I answered.

'There was a pause, then Mason said in a low voice: "Have you ever heard of Master Edward?"

'I nodded.

' "And that he is dead?" she went on.

' "Yes," I replied, "I have seen his grave."

' "Who told you about him?" said the old woman. "Did anyone tell you he killed himself?"

' "Killed himself!" I exclaimed. "Oh no, oh no. Why, he must have been only a child."

' "I don't know," said Mason. "I don't know," she went on with increasing agitation. "I have always felt sure it was an accident. The jury said it was, but why does he walk? If, poor lamb, he fell out by accident, he would be at rest in heaven, and yet he walks. You, who are a stranger to us all, have heard him. Oh, my lady, my lady, why did you drive him to it?"

'Her agitation was pitiable, and absorbed in that I seemed to forget my own fear. But, as Mason grew calmer, I determined to reach the bottom of the mystery, and at last after much persuasion and many questions I elicited from her the following story.

'Sir Arthur K. had been deeply in love with his second wife, and she had apparently returned his affection. At the time of the marriage in 1883, when Mason first came into contact with him, Edward, the child of the first wife, was six years old. He was a pretty, affectionate, spirited boy, a little inclined to be unduly sensitive, but on the whole a perfectly normal, healthy boy. Sir Arthur was much attached to him, and his stepmother treated him with the greatest kindness. This treatment continued after the births of her own two children, all three were treated as her own, and Mason declared that she as well as Sir Arthur believed Lady K. really felt an almost equal devotion to them all.

'A change came soon after the death of Sir Arthur in 1887. The bulk of Sir Arthur's estate consisted of the Wyke property, and, at the date of the first marriage, this estate had been settled on the first wife and her children. There was, therefore, little that Sir Arthur could do for the children of his second marriage, save economise and thus form a fund for their benefit, but his brief tenure of life after his second marriage precluded him from accomplishing much in that respect. It is true that he made a will bequeathing any contingent benefit in his estate to his second wife and her children, but this was all. Lady K. herself had no fortune to speak of.

'On his papers being opened after his death it was found that Sir Arthur had left his wife and an elderly clergyman, a Mr Cameron who had been an early friend of his, joint guardians of the children. Practically, this amounted to Lady K. becoming sole guardian, since Mr Cameron lived in a remote part of England, was in poor health and really took no interest whatever in his wards.

'Mason was most emphatic that at no time was actual cruelty shown the boy, but she admitted that he was neglected. He was neglected in everything, education, manners, health, companions: all that Lady K. had was lavished on her own children whilst Edward was stinted in every direction. It speaks volumes for the natural goodness of the boy that he did not grow to hate his little half-brother and sister, but to the last he was always affectionate and gentle with them, and loved their society. With his stepmother it was different. Violent disputes took place between them, battles in which the impetuous, warm-hearted, neglected child dashed himself in vain against the cold-blooded, heartless woman. Into further details we need not go. Suffice it to say that one evening there was an unusually violent outburst, which ended in Edward rushing, sobbing and distracted, up to his little attic in the wing, for to this remote corner was the future owner of Wyke Hall now exiled. In the morning a gardener found the boy lying on the stoneflagged terrace beneath his window – dead.

'There was an inquest of course, but in deference to the position of the family the inquiry made was as formal as possible. The usual verdict was returned: Death by misadventure; and Lady K. found herself in the position of own mother to the future lord of Wyke.

'But her demeanour did not change, the coldness and hardness, only melted by her children's embraces, which had been growing on her now for the past few years remained, and she shut herself off deliberately from the neighbours to live solitary with her children.

'After a while rumours began to spread: something had happened at Wyke Hall, the house was haunted. All was very vague, but servants began to leave and it became difficult to replace them. At last Lady K. called her household together in the hall and boldly broached the subject to them. Presently she challenged the assembled party.

' "Well, you say that the room my poor Edward lived in is haunted. Will you admit that you are wrong if I pass tonight alone and in peace and quiet there?"

'There was a murmur of assent.

'Lady K. was as good as her word. She passed that night alone in the attic; she left it next morning as calm and composed as ever, but, as the servants noticed, a deathly white. And in a week's time workmen came and the attics over the wing were pulled down.

'Since that date, the wing, except for the schoolroom, had not been used; I was the first person to spend a night in it since Lady K. had done so three years before.

'This was all Mason could tell me. When she had finished, she sat looking at me. ' "And now you know," she said.

'I was shaking with a mixture of fear and anger. ' "I will stay no longer than I must in this house," I answered as quietly as I could, "and I will never pass another night in that bedroom."

' "I knew you would say that," said Mason. "I will have your things moved at once to the room next to mine."

' "Thank you," I said, and left her.

'All was done as Mason had promised, and that evening saw me installed in my new room. I have never known what the servants thought of the sudden change. I said nothing to the maid, nor she to me. Nor did Lady K. make a single comment. At luncheon the next day she was calm and composed as ever; I caught her more than once eyeing me covertly, but she said nothing of note. That evening, having fully made up my mind, I handed her a note informing her that I desired to leave at the end of the term. I gave no reasons. She read my note in my presence, and in a perfectly unmoved voice said: "I shall be sorry to lose you, Miss Hosmer."

'Nothing further of the slightest interest transpired during the remainder of my stay at Wyke Hall. I was careful always to leave the schoolroom early in the evening and retire to my new room, and I heard the footsteps no more. My relations with Lady K. remained on the same cool and polite footing as ever. Occasionally I thought I saw a look of malice and fear in her eyes, but outwardly we were at peace. To the children I became really attached, and my sole regret at leaving that charming, that dreadful house, was my being parted from them. In fact, as my acquaintance with them grew, I began seriously to regret the approaching close of my relationship with them. I feared I had acted too hastily in resigning my engagement, but it was now too late to draw back. I knew Lady K.'s secret, and she knew that I knew it; to part was the only alternative.

'Many years have passed since then,' said Miss Hosmer, winding up her story, 'and I have never seen or heard of the family again. I have a vague impression that Lady K. is dead, and I pray nightly even now that the wandering spirit of that dead child whom she hunted to his grave has also found eternal rest.'

Mr Oliver Carmichael

Mr Oliver Carmichael was one of the fortunate ones of the world. Of good family, he was the late born and only child of wealthy, cultivated and affectionate parents, under whose auspices he received the orthodox and pleasant education of an English gentleman. After happy, though not especially distinguished careers at Eton and Oxford, he had obtained an excellent berth in one of our minor government offices and had there settled down to the life of a worthy, if not hard-worked Civil Servant. In addition to this occupation he had taken up as a hobby the collection of old silver, and in the pursuit of this found all the mental stimulus that he required.

Mr Carmichael was not a society man, in fact, he rather avoided the companionship of women, preferring the seclusion of one of our best and most exclusive Clubs, where he spent much of his leisure time and where he possessed a number of acquaintances of his own sex. Amongst these he was popular enough, for, although perhaps slightly effeminate and by no means fond of masculine sports, Mr Carmichael was a really good fellow, ready at all times to aid with advice or purse others less fortunate than himself.

In person he was of middle size and distinctly good-looking, though of rather slight frame and with a faint touch of the feminine in him. He was, when his peculiar experiences began, about thirty-seven years of age.

In due course of time his parents died, sincerely mourned by Oliver, who presently parted with their old London house and moved into smaller quarters, where he settled himself down to lead an easy bachelor life, waited on by a staff of old family servants, some of whom he had known all his life.

This is but a brief and imperfect sketch of Oliver Carmichael, but it is intended to portray him as he was: an easy-going, high-minded, good fellow, who had never been confronted with any serious problem in life, and whose aim was to lead a quiet and honourable existence in charity with all men.

An event was now, however, about to occur, which brought about a fundamental change in his nature and in his outlook on the world about him.

One night Mr Carmichael had a succession of unpleasant dreams. On waking in the morning, he could not recall their details, but he felt depressed and disturbed, and this depression and disturbance may have caused him to be a little less careful than usual over his toilet. For, whilst walking to his office – a custom which he kept up with meticulous care as being beneficial to his health-he suddenly became aware that he had left his pocket-handkerchief behind him. Though annoying, this was a matter easy to remedy, and Oliver sought out the nearest hosier's shop and entered it to purchase the needed article.

The day was yet young and the shop was nearly empty of customers. Mr Carmichael made his way to the counter indicated and a young woman stepped forward to serve him. Instantly he experienced a most curious and unpleasant sensation for which there was apparently no reason. He felt an instinctive and violent repulsion to the girl; he glanced at her more closely, but there was little externally to account for his feeling. The young woman appeared to be of the usual shop-girl class, modest and demure in manner and neatly and quietly dressed. She was a tall and strongly built person, apparently about twenty-five years of age and – was actually ugly. Not only were her features unprepossessing, but there was an indefinable look about them of something evil, not in any positive sense, but rather negatively; it was the look of one whose thoughts and aspirations were set on a low and maleficent plane.

Mr Carmichael purchased his handkerchief and paid for it by handing the girl a sovereign. Up to the present she had paid him no more attention than was demanded by her duties, but as she gave him his change she looked him straight in the face, and he saw, for an instant, a look of exulting triumph flash into her eyes. She instantly averted them. Oliver turned to leave the shop, feeling a faint sensation of fear, an indefinite fear of something that he could not understand. As he reached the door he turned and looked back; the girl was watching him steadily.

He proceeded on his way to the office revolving the little adventure in his mind. At first he treated it but lightly and endeavoured to analyse the cause of his sudden aversion to a perfectly respectable and civil shop-girl. But gradually he found the affair taking on a more serious aspect: the personality of the girl began to oppress him, her image kept rising before him, and it was an image presaging ill and wretchedness to himself. All day the affair haunted him and, even in the evening at his Club and during his usual quiet game of bridge after dinner, that baleful look of evil triumphant in the girl's eyes continued to obtrude itself.

When at last he went to bed and finally fell asleep he dreamed again, and this time the recollection of his vision remained with him the next day. He dreamed that he was alone on an apparently desert plain, enveloped in a luminous grey mist, which whirled round him in sweeping masses ever driven by the wind. Across this plain he was journeying, exactly whither he knew not, but filled with a set purpose to reach his unknown destination. Suddenly out of the mist a figure loomed up, which he instantly recognised as that of the shop-girl. She came towards him, her eyes gleaming with an evil joy. In wild panic he turned and fled, forgetting his destination, careless of his fate, seeking only to escape from the swift-moving figure which pursued him. The grey luminosity around him grew darker, his confusion increased, the threatening pursuer gained upon him. He woke with a cry; daylight was stealing into the room.

He rose that morning from his bed unrefreshed and still agitated over his dream. He endeavoured in the light of a new day to look at the whole episode more calmly, and gradually forced himself to believe that he had succeeded in stilling the nervous agitation that had possessed him the day before. He found himself presently walking to his office, but it was by a new, a pleasanter route as he fondly imagined; he laughed bitterly to himself as he gradually realised that he had selected this new route to avoid passing the hosier's shop. All that day the thought of the girl haunted him and at last after much reflection he decided on a new means of obliterating her memory. His annual leave was soon due, affairs at the office were quiet, he would ask his chief to permit him to forestall his holiday, and would go away at once. No sooner decided upon than done. His chief readily gave the required permission, and Mr Carmichael astonished his household by announcing on his return that evening that he was going to Brighton the following day, to remain there for a week before he proceeded on the round of quiet country-house visits which he had arranged for his regular holiday.

To Brighton Oliver Carmichael went accordingly, but change of scene did not serve to distract him from his prevailing obsession. He thought very often of the girl, of whom he now had an unutterable loathing, and he also found himself pursued by other thoughts. Hitherto his life's habits had induced in him a train of pleasant and amiable ideas, not perhaps marked by any special eminence in the way of ability, but the thoughts of a clean-minded, honourable man. Now he found himself imperceptibly drifting into other trains of thought: evil notions passed through his mind, views of humanity taken from a hostile and a wicked standpoint, impressions of the worst side of human nature obtruded themselves. He fought desperately against these new ideas, but he felt it was a losing fight; he began to lose all confidence in himself, his integrity, his honour; he began to despair.

He no longer dreamed of nights, but lay buried in profound slumber, slumber in which it may well be that the thing we call the soul may leave its earthly shell and wander to realms and seek affinities utterly unknown to our waking personalities.

Mr Carmichael, deep though his sleep might he, was now in the habit of waking unrefreshed and troubled, and though he exerted himself, both inwardly for the sake of his own peace of mind and outwardly for the sake of the conventions of life, to preserve his usual demeanour it was noticed later on by his friends that he seemed distraught and to have lost his former happy and placid content and generous instincts.

His holiday over, Mr Carmichael returned to town filled with a new resolve. He would go again and see this ill-omened girl; he persuaded himself that her haunting personality would be dissipated by another sight of her in the flesh. He had made, he said to himself, a mountain out of a molehill; because he had taken a dislike to a girl's face there was no reason that she should drive him into madness from thinking of her. A second inspection would, no doubt, show her to be just an ordinary plain-faced girl, full of her own affairs, who had never given another thought to the casual buyer of a handkerchief some weeks before. He resolved, therefore, once more to visit the shop on the pretext of making a small purchase, and, this decision being taken, he felt easier in his mind. The next morning he made the trial, and it was, it must be confessed, with a nervous although more hopeful heart that Mr Carmichael pushed opened the shop doors and entered.

His first glance around did not disclose the girl, but when he had approached the well-remembered counter she stepped forward quietly to meet him. As before she moved modestly and demurely; she glanced casually at him, her manner was that of an absolute and totally indifferent stranger. Carmichael felt reassured, he was right: he had made a fool of himself, the girl had never thought of him and did not now even remember him.

She asked him his needs. Mr Carmichael hesitated and then blundered out the first thing he could think of. Gloves. She produced them and asked him his size; Mr Carmichael had forgotten, his valet usually bought such articles for him. Then she must measure his hand.

He held it out and she stooped to her slight task. As she stretched the glove across his hand she touched it with her own, momentarily, perhaps accidentally. The touch sent a shock as of electricity through him, all his self-possession vanished, all his belief in the unreality of the past few weeks. For one blinding instant he saw into deeps hitherto unsuspected and sensed a horror hitherto undreamt of. Scarcely knowing what he did he took the gloves, paid for them and stood for a moment looking at the girl.

So far her manner had been that of the shop assistant, doing her work carefully and politely but somewhat mechanically; she had shown no trace of recognition or of any sense of understanding. Suddenly she raised her eyes and looked straight into his own and once more he saw a blaze of exultation, a look of power light them up. She knew herself mistress of the situation; she knew and understood the secret links that bound him to her, links that he felt dimly controlled him, but the nature of which he could not comprehend.

All this passed in a moment, the girl averted her eyes and turned carelessly from him; Mr Carmichael left the shop almost unmanned. He reached his office, but was utterly incapable of concentrating his mind upon his work, and presently his chief, seeing him to be unwell, advised him to go home. Mr Carmichael leapt at the idea, he would go back to the shop, he felt he must go back to the shop, he would see her again, he felt he must see her again; perhaps she would explain things, perhaps he would see his way clearer. He put on his hat and left the office.

But on arrival at the shop he was doomed to disappointment; it was early closing day and all the assistants had gone home. He walked on towards his own house, in a state of mingled disappointment and relief. He felt he must see her, and yet he dreaded the interview; he knew it would be a decisive one, but how he would emerge from it he felt to be uncertain.

He found himself drawing near home and passing through one of our quiet London squares. As he turned a corner of it, he met his enemy, for so he felt the girl to be, face to face.

She was walking quietly towards him, neatly and modestly dressed, demure as ever in her expression, but with perhaps a shade of anxiety in it also. As they approached each other, she raised her eyes. There was no blaze of triumph in them now, they were deep and watchful as they rested on his face. Almost unconsciously he raised his hat; she acknowledged the salute and the next moment found him walking on beside her.

For a few minutes silence reigned, then Mr Carmichael, collecting himself, began: 'I am glad to have met you, I was anxious to see you, I went by Messrs — and found the shop shut.' He paused.

'Yes?' said the other interrogatively.

'I do not understand things,' went on Oliver. 'Ever since that day nearly five weeks ago when I came into the shop to buy a handkerchief, I have been haunted by you. I have thought of you waking, I have, I know it now, been possessed by you in sleep.' Again he paused.

'Are you trying to make love to me?' said the girl with a short laugh.

This notion so astounded Mr Carmichael that for an instant he was struck dumb. Then he ejaculated: 'Love! Make love to you! Oh, Heaven forbid!'

'You are not very polite,' said his companion. 'Well, if you are not moved by love, perhaps you are moved by its opposite, and you hate me.'

She looked keenly at him, and Mr Carmichael hesitated for a reply. She went on: 'You need not trouble to mince matters. I know your feelings, know them far better than you do yourself.'

By this time their wanderings had led them into the Park and the girl, motioning towards two vacant chairs, said: 'Let us sit down, there may be much to speak of.'

He complied without answering her and looked long and fixedly at her. As always, she looked calm, demure and mistress of herself; only in her eyes there burned a sombre light, powerful, mysterious, menacing. She turned away.

'What has happened to me?' he said. 'Who are you, what do you want of me? I am at sea.'

She answered slowly: 'You have asked several questions, the full answers to which you are not yet fit to understand, but I will tell you something. Who am I? Well, you will find out some day who and what I really am, but you may now call me by the name my parents gave me, Phyllis Rourke; I was not always, even here, what I now am, a shop-girl. My father was a man of wisdom, a gentleman who taught me how to learn' – she hesitated – 'many things, truths, facts, which are obscure to you and all your like. What do I want of you? Well, much, and much that you will dread to part with, but I hold you' – she detached a blossom from her dress and held it in her hand – 'like I hold this flower, and I can crush you as I do it.'

She suited her actions to her words and sat silently gazing at the ruined flower. Mr Carmichael struggled between fear and anger. Who was this boastful girl, he thought; was he not a gentleman, a man of position, what had he really to fear from the threats of an unknown girl from a second-class shop?

Summoning up his courage he answered: 'These are fine words, Miss Rourke, but you do not consider what I may do in the meantime. You indulge in threats to persecute me? Have you considered our relative social positions? Do you know I am Mr Carmichael and a man of influence and reputation? In the last place have you considered – the police? Persons who annoy others are apt to find themselves in trouble.'

He spoke more bravely than he felt. As the words passed his lips he felt his courage evaporating. She listened unmoved, smiling, with something of the air of a cat watching a mouse.

When he had finished, she waited a few moments and then in a low, intensely concentrated voice answered: 'Oh, you poor fool! How little you understand. Since that night five weeks ago when first I found you, before you saw my living face, have you learned nothing? You talk of your position, of your social influence; you prate of the police.' Her eyes, dark and gloomy, seemed to devour him as she went on: 'What can you do? I hold you and shall always hold you. I may never see you again in this body, I want nothing of your material life, I want something more, I want you yourself, I want your soul.'

He shrank back in horror. 'Are you the Devil?' he said.

She burst into a fit of terrible, silent laughter. 'The Devil,' she said, 'we are becoming quite mediaeval. Do you expect to see this foot,' and she pushed forward her own, 'turned into a hoof?

Are you waiting for me to take out a parchment to be signed in your blood?'

She laughed again. 'No, Mr Carmichael,' she went on, 'I am not the Devil. Perhaps you would be better off if I were.'

There was a silence. Mr Carmichael felt like a bird in the presence of a snake. He was fascinated, he was filled with abhorrence: he wished to fly, he could not; he wished to fortify his spirit to resist, he felt it yielding and becoming more and more plastic under the influence of her personality.

Presently she spoke again. 'There is no more to be said now,' she began, 'we have talked long enough. You understand as much as you are yet fitted to understand: you know now what you but feared before, that I control you, control you for a purpose clear to myself, if not to you. We need not meet again, I shall summon you when I choose and you will come to me when I call you in the places of sleep.'

Another shock passed through Oliver Carmichael. Like a lightning flash there passed across him the knowledge that in those deep sleeps he had had recently his soul, detached from his body, communed with that of Phyllis Rourke amidst strange and terrible surroundings. He resolved he must try not to sleep again; she answered his thought with a laugh.

'Oh yes,' she said, 'you will sleep as well as ever. And now,' she added, 'it is time to part. I live with my aunt in Fulham and the old soul will wonder where I am.'

She rose from her chair. 'Goodbye, Mr Carmichael,' she said. '*Au revoir*, my dear affinity, till tonight.'

She left him and Oliver remained sitting dazed, helpless and despairing, till a park keeper warned him of the closing gates.

Mr Carmichael returned home in a state verging on stupefaction; the amazing conversation which had taken place, the force and malevolent disposition of Phyllis Rourke appalled him. He felt, as before said, like a bird fascinated by a snake, he desired to struggle, to escape from the toils which were closing round him, but no avenue presented itself. Vainly he racked his brains and vainly he tried to summon up will-power sufficient to effect – he scarcely knew what. He was threatened from a quarter totally unguarded and by dangers the very existence of which he had never hitherto suspected. And he was threatened by what? That again he did not know. Tangible evils affecting his life or his possessions he would have known how to face or to endeavour to face, but this was an evil affecting his soul. Like many other people who have always led smooth and peaceful lives, the problems of the soul had never disturbed him. He was vaguely conscious of its existence, he had in his youth been an orthodox member of the English Church, but of late years he had slipped imperceptibly into a mild form of agnosticism and, while always ready to offer a helping hand to those needing his assistance, he had never really given any consideration to the problems of suffering or wrong. He had sought to avoid them; he knew of their existence, but only after an ill-defined fashion, and he had endeavoured to retain his own happy calm by minimising them and hiding them from his consciousness as far as possible.

Now all was changed in an instant. He found himself in the grip of what seemed to him Evil incarnate. He knew the mind of the girl to be as fertile a field for evil as he had hitherto imagined his own to be for good. And he was powerless to resist her. What would become of him? Was she destined to drag him down to her own low plane and destroy that entity, his soul, which he now for the first time began clearly to realise existed?

He thought and thought, but little help came to him. Only one way finally illumined his darkness and this he well realised might prove a will-o'-the-wisp. The girl had threatened to seek him out in sleep. Well, he would turn night into day, he would watch at night and rest in the daylight hours, when he fondly imagined that she would be attending to her waking duties. Somewhat encouraged at having at least found a chance of salvation, he passed through the rest of the evening endeavouring to collect and control himself and at the usual hour for going to rest he made up his fire and selecting a book settled down to his nocturnal vigil.

But he found it impossible to concentrate on the printed page. His thoughts wandered to Phyllis Rourke. What was she doing, was she triumphing over him, was she even now striving to approach him? He tried to dismiss these thoughts; he resumed his book.

*   *   *

He woke with a start. The fire was out, the lamp had died down, daylight streamed into the room and he fancied as he regained his consciousness he heard Phyllis Rourke's low, mocking laugh.

*   *   *

This night was the beginning of despair for Oliver Carmichael. His hope for protection against his unseen assailant had failed him and he knew of no other help.

To detail the events of the next few months would be as difficult as useless; to the end of his life Oliver Carmichael looked back upon them as a descent into bell itself. It will suffice to summarise his experiences briefly. After his one effort at an all-night vigil he decided it was useless to attempt to vary his ordinary form of life and he returned to it and lived it as heretofore. Dealing first with this external existence, it may be said, that his acquaintances found him gradually changing; the differences were not very marked, but it was noticed that he did not take quite his old placid, kindly view of human nature. His judgment grew more bitter, he became prone to attribute bad motives rather than good to the actions of others; his good temper became less marked, his desire to help others faded, he became selfish, cold, unmerciful. Socially, he became more ambitious; he frequented parties, he entertained at home, but although he thus joined more in the life of the body politic, yet he was less popular than of old. His more intimate friends grieved over the change in him, endeavoured to reason with him and, failing to convince, drew gradually away from him. In his work he did well and earned the approbation, without increasing the affection, of his colleagues. So much for the outer Mr Carmichael. It will be harder to paint the inner man.

At first he fought desperately against the hated invasion of his personality, but from the first he felt it to be a losing fight. He was unarmed and blinded against the attack of a skilled and watchful foe. In his waking hours he was never conscious of any hostile presence. Night and she were his enemies. He rested soundly, never dreaming, or rather never being able to recall his dreams. And yet he was well aware that it was during sleep that his soul, torn from his body by the powerful spirit of Phyllis Rourke, was dragged, resisting hopelessly, through the mire of spiritual degradation. He knew this, and nightly he summoned up his forces to this losing battle and daily realised he had taken another step on the downward path.

It is, perhaps, not accurate to say that his struggles were renewed every night; it is impossible to say, but it is certain that on some nights the battle was fiercer than on others, since he would wake on certain mornings, trembling, weary and bathed in perspiration, as if indeed he had but just emerged from a frightful ordeal. And he noticed that after each one of these dreadful nights he made a very distinct step forward in his knowledge and love of evil. His love of evil! It was with a frightful pang that once, when meditating on his fate and bemoaning his lost innocence, a still, small voice spoke within him, 'With lost innocence you have gained knowledge.' The thought had dwelt with him and slowly he had begun to realise that, deep within himself, he had begun to prefer vice to virtue, evil to good.

Ever since the hated invasion of his sleeping personality had begun, Oliver Carmichael had striven his hardest to repel the invader. He was, as we know, a man of high principles, if not of strong will, and his waking consciousness, aware of the hostile influences acting on his soul, had set itself to resist these influences as resolutely as possible, and at first during his daylight hours with no little success. Even up to that moment he had believed that these horrible thoughts were forced upon him and were external to his real self; he now perceived that on the contrary they formed part of himself and were knit into him inextricably. Phyllis Rourke had done her work well; she had not only captured his pure soul with her evil one, but she had even intermingled her wicked personality with his so that her thoughts and his own had become one, and it was impossible for him to decide whether the impulses and reasons which guided him were his own or hers. He had lost his identity together with his principles.

This last blow seemed likely to crush him. Hitherto he had vaguely hoped that death at any rate would put a period to his sufferings, and he had from time to time even dwelt on thoughts of suicide to escape from them. He had been restrained from this last step by a vague recollection of earlier religious training and by a fear that by violating a moral law he might end by making his condition worse. All hope of final relief, however, was now cut off, he had lost himself, he was one for ever with his evil genius.

*   *   *

Six months of mental and spiritual anguish elapsed and during this time Oliver Carmichael never felt the faintest desire again to see his tormentor, nor did her presence force itself upon him during his waking hours. It was only subconsciously that he was aware of her approach to him during sleep, though he never doubted that she was the cause and formed the larger part of his misery. But he would pass the shop of Messrs — , where he presumed her still to be employed, without concern and without ever desiring to ascertain whether Phyllis Rourke was still to be found there. Nor had he made any enquiries about her, her relation to him had no connection with the things of this world, but lay, as he well knew now, entirely on another plane.

This was the position when, about six months after the first meeting between Mr Carmichael and Miss Rourke, the former awoke one morning with the well-known signs of his nocturnal battle upon him. He was tired, trembling, bathed in perspiration, but somewhere deep within him he felt a new sensation, a sense of exhilaration; in that awful battle of the souls he had for once proved victorious. He knew it, though he knew nothing else, for throughout his long period of suffering, it must be carefully remembered, he never knew the details of those nightly happenings: he knew the results, not the causes.

Strangely gladdened he rose from his bed and dressed himself, meditating as he did so on what had happened, and even now vaguely beginning to hope that his trials might yet come to an end, and that he would, through the aid of some unknown power, be able to tear Phyllis Rourke from his personality. The day passed more happily than any had done since his first visit to the shop and on his homeward way he felt an impulse towards entering it and seeking out his enemy. He did not do so, however.

That night he dreamed, and on this occasion the dream remained with him at waking. He dreamed that he was himself again and walking in a fair country. Overhead the sun shone brightly, its rays tempered by a gentle breeze. Birds sang in the trees and hedgerows, rabbits played on the short turf and myriads of wild flowers blossomed and scented the air. In front of him a pair of lovers were strolling, arms interlocked, evidently out for a happy day. All was peaceful and serene and he walked onwards, cheery, good tempered and feeling in charity with all men. Suddenly he heard a cry, the singing of the birds was hushed, a hawk had swooped and borne off a hapless little creature in its clutches. The sight was unpleasant and marred the peaceful scene; he turned away his eyes, *he* was not to blame, it was Nature. At that moment there was a shrill scream, a stoat had sprung upon one of the rabbits, it clung to its neck viciously biting under the ear of the little beast, which struggled vainly to shake off its deadly rider. Mr Carmichael shuddered; scenes of blood and violence were repulsive to him; he hurried on. But the wind had dropped, the heat had become oppressive, the wild flowers, withering under the glare of the sun, drooped their heads. The beauty of the landscape faded, its outlines were still there, but they were obscured and blurred by a mist, like those which, rising from the sea, instantaneously blot out the distant, sunlit shipping. He turned a corner of the road; again he saw the lovers, but they had quarrelled, high words were passing between them; on seeing Mr Carmichael's approach they hurried on, but their angry voices came back to his ears. Now the clouds had gathered, the sun was obscured, the heat was stifling; suddenly the storm burst, the thunder rolled, the lightning flashed and rain fell in torrents. Mr Carmichael sheltered himself and, the fury of the storm quickly passing over, he resumed his way. Refreshed by the rain the wild flowers again raised their heads and perfumed the air, the birds sang, and before him the lovers, reconciled, pursued their happy way. Trouble had come and had passed. He woke.

That morning among his letters he found one in a handwriting strange to him, but of whose authorship he had no doubts. It was from Phyllis Rourke. He hesitated for a few moments then, opening it, he read as follows.

Dear Mr Carmichael,
I greatly wish to see you again, if it be possible. Tomorrow I leave Messrs — early and shall walk in the Park near where I met you before. I shall be there by 4 p.m. and will wait.

Yours sincerely,
Phyllis Rourke

P.S. Do come.

Mr Carmichael felt no surprise at this letter. He knew now that he had expected it to come, but he was doubtful as to what course to follow. Miss Rourke evidently wanted to see him. Why should he do anything to oblige Miss Rourke? His anger against her rose, she was his worst enemy. He looked at the matter from another aspect. He glanced at himself in the glass, and saw himself a handsome, well groomed gentleman; it might be well to go and show Miss Phyllis that, at any rate, her evil deeds had not harmed his body. Undecided, he went to his office, and he was still undecided when he set out on his walk home after lunch. Almost unconsciously he found himself in the Park and near the well-remembered spot where he had talked with Miss Rourke six months before. He found two chairs, sat down and waited, and presently saw her coming towards him.

His heart throbbed with mingled excitement, fear and hatred. As she drew near he looked at her attentively and saw that she was somehow changed: her features were less harsh than formerly, her eyes looked softer; in her dress she was as always neat and modest. She approached him quickly and quietly, there was pleasure in her face at seeing him. He rose from his seat and waited for her.

'I am glad you have come,' she said, omitting any more formal greeting, 'very glad. There are things I have to say to you, knowledge I must impart.'

He looked coldly at her. 'What can you have to say to me?' he began. 'Do you realise what you have done to me: to me who never injured you, to me a stranger to you, a harmless stranger, who sought but to live his life in peace?'

'I know what has happened,' she answered 'and my knowledge goes further than your own. I know what you have suffered and the change that has come about in you.' She stopped.

There was a short silence, then she resumed: 'But if I know what has happened to you you are ignorant as to what has taken place in myself.'

'I am indifferent as to that,' said Mr Carmichael. 'What have you to do with me?'

She laughed a little, but not the mocking laugh he knew so well, and said: 'When you know all you will not say that; but now look at me, can you see any change in me?'

Carmichael looked at her. 'Yes,' he said slowly, 'you are changed.' He hesitated. 'You are changed – for the better,' he went on.

She smiled again. 'I am changed,' she said, 'and for the better, and this I owe to you. In the struggle that has taken place between us, I have gained much and perhaps you have lost – nothing.'

'I do not understand you,' said he.

She turned again and looked steadily at him. As he gazed at her a new man woke within him. He saw as in a glass darkly the blurred outlines of a mighty truth; he essayed to focus it, to make clear to his mind that which his subconscious self already perceived.

But he failed, the vision faded, he sighed and said, varying his previous words: 'I cannot understand you.'

'Not yet,' she answered, 'not yet. Your inner, your true vision is still clouded by the workings of your earthly mind. You cannot yet see clearly those wonderful affinities that exist between the souls of those we wrongly call individuals. Just as darkness and light combined make the perfect day, so do the intermingled spirits of man and woman form one perfect whole. Separated in past ages, as darkness and light were separated, for some mysterious purpose, the divided souls now seek each other throughout the ages, striving once more to unite. Some happy ones have achieved their purpose, although, clouded by earthly and external thoughts, they are as yet but dimly conscious of their triumph, but most are still seekers wandering in the night.'

'I begin to understand you,' he said.

'Of those seekers,' she went on, 'I was one, and one of not the least wretched. In times far beyond our ken, Fate, Chance, what you will, severed our knit souls, and set yours on the paths of peace and joy, whilst, I, ill-fated, was turned towards the lower depths. I do not know how long I sought you, but I know that through the ages I sought in vain, and slowly there grew up in my inmost deeps a hatred of you, my joint spirit, a hatred bred of envy and despair. At last I found you, before ever you saw me in the flesh I found you in the spirit – and when you came that first day to the shop, my soul rejoiced, for I knew that I had succeeded and that you were mine. Then I began my work, to drag you down and plunge you into the abyss of those lost souls, wherein I felt myself to be. I sought to blacken you.' She paused, and after a few moments, went on in a lower voice: But I forgot that black mingled with white forms grey, and that grey may at last bleach in the sunlight to purest white.'

There was a long silence; slowly the truth possessed him, the knowledge already buried in him arose and, passing through his consciousness, filled him with content.

'I think I understand you,' he said.

Phyllis went on: 'And now the fight was joined and triumphantly I watched your struggles, your slow fall. Joy possessed me, the joy of evil victorious, but gradually with that joy ill ease mingled. Gradually, imperceptibly to myself even, my onslaughts slackened, and your resistance increased. Of those dreadful, silent battles of the night your earthly sense knows nothing, but even before that recent morning when you awoke victorious I knew that I had failed and, failing, I rejoiced. As you sank, I rose and, rising, helped you to rise again.'

Again she stopped and again went on: 'Now you know all, and now you know that, separated once, we are once more knit together for ever. In this existence we shall meet no more, it will be better so, but do you go back and take up your daily life, your work, resume your friends, rejoin your family, if you have one. As for me, a small legacy has come to me, and I have persuaded my aunt to leave London and live with me in the country, where I can pass this life in quiet and thought. We have both a battle still before us, you to regain, I to attain, merit, but let us both strive after that knowledge which brings Peace, which is God.'

Again there was silence, then she rose and held out her hand. 'Goodbye, Mr Carmichael,' she said. 'Goodbye.'

He rose also and held her hand an instant. '*Au revoir*,' he said, 'till we meet again in sleep.'

They parted and went upon their separate ways.